BROKEN
dove

A simple arrangement. A complicated future.

www.chellebliss.com

CHELLE BLISS

USA TODAY BESTSELLING AUTHOR

LIA

"LIA, ARE YOU AWAKE?"

I hear Leo's voice calling to me in my dreams, and I bury my face deeper in the pillow.

"Lia?"

The familiar squeak of my bedroom door opening lets me know the voice is real.

"Leo, it's *early*…" I groan.

As soon as I stir and speak, the dogs scramble from their hiding place under my blankets and leap off my bed to greet Leo.

"You asked me to wake you up before I go," he reminds me.

I can hear the jangling of the dogs' collars as the three jockey for the best position, which means the most contact with Leo's hands. I understand that feeling.

I squint against the weak light and can barely make out Leo Hawk, my roommate of over a year, kneeling in the doorway.

He must be fresh out of the shower because I can smell the soap he uses. None of that fake, metallic man-smell for him.

I pry my eyes open and roll over to greet him properly.

"Sweet Jesus, Lia," he says, rubbing his forehead and tearing his eyes away from me and my bare flesh.

I curl my lips into a sleepy grin. "You know I sleep naked, bud. You wake me up, you're asking for the full show."

I can't help it if I like teasing him. Smelling him so fresh and seeing him all dressed for the day sends my body into overdrive. Without even realizing it, my nipples go hard, and I rub my thighs together under the sheets.

"I-I know…" he stutters, looking away. "I just… I uh…"

God, I love my roommate. All tattooed, grease monkey, biker guy on the outside, but on the inside, the dude is pure mush. Sweet and gooey. Easy to

2

tease, and even easier to distract. I'm having the time of my life living with him.

"Is this a full-contact wake-up call?" I ask. "Or do you need to be on your way?"

"Fuuuuuuck," Leo says, his voice thick and needy. "I have shit to do this morning. You do too, remember? The phone interview."

The way I torture him is almost cruel. I know damn well what he's got on his schedule today. He's been a prospect for the MC for almost a year now, and my dad and the other guys keep him busy. The very same MC that my dad happens to be the president of.

"Hmmm." I pat the bed beside me. "How long do we need?"

"Not long," he says, with that expression he gets when he's torn up about something.

He doesn't admit it, but being in the club means everything to him. I don't want to screw that up for him. But morning sex...

"I can work with 'not long,'" I remind him.

"Your dad wants me to—" He flicks a glance at his phone, checking the time.

"Leo," I say, a warning in my voice, "did you just bring up my dad while I'm waiting for you to

3

decide whether or not you have time to fuck me before you leave for the day?"

He swallows in that adorably sexy way he has, pressing his lips together and lifting his brows. Leo looks down at his clothes. "Let's focus on the fucking and not on the other part."

"Forget it. It's all right," I say, rolling onto my back. I bend my knees so the sheets tent over my legs. I slide one hand under the sheet. "If you're in a rush, I'll take care of myself this morning."

I bring my other hand to my breast and tweak my nipple between two fingers. It doesn't feel anywhere near as good as when Leo does it, though.

He watches me, his dark eyes flaring even in the low light. I squirm a little under the sheets, so he knows I'm doing something down there too.

He tosses his plain white T-shirt over his head and kicks off his work boots.

Finally, I get what I want.

"Fuck it," he mutters. "If your da—if the guys are gonna have my ass, at least I can have yours first."

I whoop with delight and pull back the covers to welcome him into bed.

He unfastens his pants and stands in his bare

feet, a raging erection already tenting his boxers. "First things first," he says, and kneels again. "Come on, girls," he says, waving my dogs toward the door. "You know the drill. Don't need an audience."

He shoos the girls out and closes the door gently behind them. We'd tried fucking with the dogs in the room before but learned the hard way that two was company, but two people and three dogs made an incredibly awkward crowd.

Leo strides over to the bed and is under the covers with me in seconds. "You kill me, you know that?" he asks.

"Me?" I smirk at him. "I love you, Leo. I would never kill you." I don't even flinch at the word, but shit…he does.

But I like this.

What we have is fun.

The kind of weird intimacy that comes when you live with a hot guy is something I haven't had before. But this whole friends with a little fucking thrown in is awesome. We *sleep* together but never sleep together. Separate rooms, separate beds, except when we share mine or his for a little while.

I like this arrangement, and I think Leo's happy.

If the orgasms we share every week are any indication, this setup works for both of us quite nicely.

The gravity of what I said hits me suddenly. I do love Leo, and he knows it, doesn't he? I tell him all the time.

I love everything about Leo, and I do "love" him. But the L-word in all caps... That's not what this is, and as long as we keep it simple, we can keep on having fun.

That's my motto in life and in relationships —*love* everyone. But at the same time, *LOVE* no one.

Before his dick wilts, I have to recharge the energy in the room, so I reach down for a breast and lift it toward him.

"Want me to lick them, or do you want a turn?" My smile or—let's be real—the way I'm kneading my tit in my hand brings Leo back to the moment.

"Me," he huffs, and in an instant, Leo's mouth is clamped on my nipple.

He starts out gentle, sucking lightly against my skin in a steady rhythm that turns my core to molten heat. The tip of his tongue teases me in torturous flicks that he alternates with the pinch of his teeth. His beautiful, perfect mouth knows how to scrape against me until I'm writhing, pushing my chest hard against his face, wanting more.

I moan a greedy sound, giving him lots of encouragement. "Fuck, Leo, yes… God, you know exactly what I need."

I close my eyes and disappear into the haze of pleasure, groping with my hands to find the solid mass of Leo's body. He's lying beside me, and while he works my breasts, I run my hands through his hair, tugging lightly with my fists without pulling his face from my body. I stroke his neck and feel the cords of his back as I grow more and more desperate.

"Leo," I pant.

My God, the way he sucks me, I swear I could come from his mouth on my tits. But he slips a hand between our bodies and kneads his way from my hips to my thighs until his hand grazes the mound of my pussy.

"Yes," I beg. "Please, baby. Don't make me wait for it."

Without another word, he slides two fingers across my seam, wetting the tips of his fingers enough so they slide deliciously over my clit. He works his fingers perfectly until I'm thrashing against the bed, begging for him to fuck me.

"Please, Leo. How do you want me?" I ask.

"Every way," he grunts.

What Leo does to me, I can't explain. When we're together, it's as close to perfection as I've ever felt.

The smell of his skin, the friction of his beard against my neck. I want to scream and ride wave after wave of pleasure, but I need to give first. Because once he takes me there, I'll be useless, and I know it. "Wait," I say.

I roll to my knees and wait while Leo settles himself on his back. His dick is rock hard and stabs the air as he leans back. I stroke the velvet skin and bend down to give it a little kiss. "Good morning, my friend," I say lightly, humming the words against the tip.

Leo sucks in a breath but doesn't speak as I stick my fingers in my mouth and wet them. I stroke his balls, running my damp fingers along the tight skin and farther underneath until Leo grates out, "Fuck, Lia."

"You will," I assure him.

I turn to give him a nice, close view of my ass and straddle him, my face toward his feet. I inch my body back toward his face so I can lower my head and take his entire length. I hold my mouth open and clamp down gently, lapping my tongue along every vein, every ridge, every inch of him.

Leo grips the sheets in his fists, but I keep up my pace, sucking and licking.

"Lia," he moans.

"Mmm," I hum, not quite ready for this quickie to end. "Almost there," I say. And I am.

I am so close to climaxing that I know once I slide down onto him, it'll be a matter of seconds, and he can be off to work. But I want a few more minutes in this happy place before I let him go.

I knead the long, tight muscles of his thighs with my fingers while I work my mouth on his cock; deeper, slower, faster. I quietly reach over to my bedside table and grab a condom from the drawer. I keep licking and sucking him while I tear open the package. Lightning-quick, I lift my head, sheathe him, and position his dick between my legs.

I lean all the way forward on my hands and knees so he gets the full view of my ass. My legs are spread wide as I kneel, and I rub the drenched tip of his cock back and forth against my clit.

He mutters incomprehensible little grunts punctuated by panting breaths until finally, I'm so close, I slide his cock inside me inch by inch, making sure I lift my ass high enough so he hits all the right angles going in.

But this morning, Leo surprises me.

Once I settle him far inside, he sits upright, his cock still planted deep.

"Move," he demands.

I do as he says, rolling my hips and working my pelvis while he reaches forward to twist my nipples so hard, I come in a dramatic, sudden crush of a climax, quicker than ever.

"Oh, fuck yes!" I scream, the pleasure knocking out my ability to see and hear. My body soft and yet tight all at once, trembling, shaking, words and sounds crashing out of me at once.

He slowly releases my nipples as I come down, and he grips my hips and leans us both back against the bed without even pulling out.

He is on his back, and I'm on top of him, the connection between us still rock hard inside me as he starts to thrust beneath me.

I don't know how he can move so fast with all my weight on him, but he is pounding me, bouncing my body with his, and before I know it, I'm coming all over him, a flood of arousal mixing with his as we both scream and hit a glorious orgasm together.

I'm sweating, panting, and lying on his chest, staring up at the ceiling. Leo's hands rest lightly on my belly.

"You may need another shower," I say, giggling through the haze of pleasure.

Leo groans but doesn't say a word as I move my weight off him and settle beside him on the bed. I reach for the bedside table and grab a fistful of tissues to blot off his dick.

"You first," I say, "you're the one who has to leave early."

"Fuck," he moans, his eyes closed. "Don't let me fall asleep."

I lie next to him for a moment, watching as his breathing evens out. A light mist of sweat has dampened his hair, but he still smells fresh and sweet.

This close to him, I can appreciate the pretty curve of his lips, with the close-trimmed beard making me want to kiss him even though he looks barely conscious.

"Such a cutie," I say.

"I luff you, Lia," he says before breaking into a soft snore.

What's that now? He said what? The words startle me upright. He loves me? Does he mean that, or is that the come-soaked ranting of a guy who is practically comatose? Why would he say that?

The words coming out of his mouth, whether he means them or not, give me feelings. Complicated feelings. And I don't do complicated.

"Wake up," I say suddenly, shoving him harder than I mean to.

His eyes fly open, and he shoots to sitting. "Fuck, what time is it?"

"It's okay," I assure him, softening my hand on his arm. "I didn't want you falling asleep."

"No, no, I'm up." He's saying the words, but his features are soft, and he looks like he's just—well, fucked someone senseless. He gets out of bed and lifts his jeans from the floor, rummaging in the pockets to find his phone. "Ah, Goddamn it," he mutters.

He bends over and gathers up his clothes and boots, giving me quite a view of his tight ass.

"You gonna make it on time?" I ask, settling back on my side to watch him.

"Yeah," he says, clutching his clothes in a ball, and walks back to the bed to give me a quick peck on the lips. "Thanks, Lia," he says.

And just like that, I can tell our roommates with bennies dynamic is back.

Balanced and stabilized.

"I'm going to shower really fast. If I roll into the

club smelling like sex, your father is literally going to murder me."

"My daddy'll murder you dead," I call out, agreeing in a lighthearted voice.

He turns and heads toward the bedroom door, giving me another awesome view of his bare ass as he leaves. "Want the girls back in?" he asks, turning unexpectedly.

He must have caught me staring because there's a hint of a flush creeping along his cheeks. I can make out the unmistakable coloring the skin above his beard.

"Hmmm-mmm," I say, appreciating his body, and because I know he can see me, I nod. "But turn back around. Don't deprive me of the show."

Leo turns and looks back at me and gives me a little shake of his head and a grin. The moment he opens my door, three panting ladies stampede back into the bedroom and nearly smush me as they jump back in bed.

"I'll see you later at work," he says. "Don't forget your call is at nine, Lia. You told me not to let you flake out."

"I won't flake," I say, acting all easy-breezy until he closes the door. "Thanks for the wake-up call."

I listen to the sounds of the shower turning on

and release a long, sleepy sigh. My body is starting to cool down, and for once, I wonder how it would be if Leo stayed. Called in sick to whatever stuff the club makes prospects do to earn their trust before they're invited to become fully patched members. But those are complicated thoughts. More time with Leo, more than mutual pleasure.... That spells complicated. I mean, I've already had a lifetime's worth of complicated in my short life, so no thanks.

Simple sex.

Simple life.

That's all I want, all I need.

All I'm willing to offer.

I pet my dogs and watch the sun illuminate my room until I hear Leo clomp down the stairs, shouting, "Later, Lia!"

Once I hear his motorcycle fire up and leave the garage, I take one last deep breath. The smells of Leo and sex surround me. I flop onto my belly and smash my face against my beat-up pillow. I close my eyes and convince myself it's time to get out of bed.

Stop thinking.

Stop feeling.

Because what I feel about Leo doesn't matter.

People come and they go.

Relationships are like seasons—the beginning is

always interesting and new, but after a few months, you're ready for the change. For what comes next.

Although, even as I think it, I remember I'm not living in a place that really has seasons anymore. I've been in Florida for a little over a year now, and the entire time has been like one extended vacation.

Some days are breezy and beautiful, others rainy, some blistering hot. But they all kind of mix together in a stew of pretty much the same.

And I love it here.

Seasonless stew and all.

So, what does that mean for my theories about relationships?

Nothing.

Not a darned thing.

Florida is my home for now.

Leo is my roommate for today.

There is a wide-open uncharted day ahead of me.

A day that's meant to be lived, and I'm about to take a major step for myself.

A new career.

New horizons.

Anything can happen, and I want to be ready to live it to the fullest as it comes.

And that's the way it needs to stay.

2

LEO

"YO, PROSPECT."

I hear Dog's familiar twang hollering at me across the lot as I roll my bike to a stop.

"Hey, man." I park in the spot designated for prospects, even though, at the moment, I'm the only one. I give Dog a chin lift, returning his welcome.

Of all the guys, Dog has been the most welcoming besides Morris.

Morris helped me, I helped Morris, and through it all, we ended up earning each other's respect—even becoming friends. When the dust settled with his old lady Alice, I had a job, became a prospect with the club, and had a new roommate in Lia.

16

Lia...I shake my head to clear the fuck fog that woman left me in.

Thank God I have about an hour's worth of shit to do here before my meeting with her dad. Sporting a semi while in a sit-down with Tiny would be the fastest way to get the prospect patch ripped right off my vest. Not to mention a punch to the throat or even worse.

I follow Dog into the club where Midge and Sadie are standing in the kitchen drinking coffee, gossiping like they always do.

"Hey, gorgeous," Sadie says, tossing me her signature smirk. "And Dog."

Sadie is what the guys call a club whore. I'd never refer to her that way, but she sure has made the rounds with most of them. She's got a good fifteen years on me—or maybe she just looks that way. It's hard to tell, and I don't ask. I learned months ago not to encourage Sadie unless I wanted to find her naked on my doorstep one day. And I sure as fuck don't want that.

"Morning," I say, keeping any inflection that could be construed as flirting out of my voice. "Midge," I say, nodding.

"Baby biker's here," Midge says, giving me a

wink. "The toilets are gonna be scrubbed real good this morning."

If Sadie's a club whore, Midge is like the club grandma and was in Sadie's place years earlier. She's got a face like a deflated walnut, but her heart's mostly in the right place. Her specialties are making shitty casseroles and putting up with our crap. But she's part of the club, which means she's family. I know she banged her share of bikers in her day, but now she mostly cooks for the guys and gets paid to do some light cleaning and the shopping.

"Baby biker," I laugh. "Midge, I would never take toilet duty off your hands. I'm gonna leave that crap to you today."

Midge raises a brow at me and pours a dash of something that smells like vanilla into her coffee. "Not today, sweet lips. Your list of shit to do today means Midge gets the day off. I might even get me a mani-pedi while you're elbows-deep in Tiny's toilet."

Sadie crows and cracks up, while Dog shakes his head with a grin on his face.

I almost never get hazed anymore, but as a prospect, fuck... Everyone makes sure I feel the pain of being at the bottom of the proverbial totem pole.

Having an older brother, I'm used to being shit on and getting leftovers and hand-me-downs, but prospecting an MC is next level.

Tim, my brother, is the reason I know Morris at all. My older brother's love affair with pills and God only knows what else nearly cost me everything.

Thanks to Tim, the building we lost was bought by the club, and Morris hired me back to work at the same auto shop my family used to own. So, while Tim cost us the building, I have a job and I didn't lose the house, so I pretty much owe my life to Morris and the club.

But I don't feel as if I'm in anybody's debt.

Being a prospect is a formality.

This is my new family, and I've never been more grateful to have someplace to belong. Someone to belong to.

Doing what I do around this place can take up a lot of time, but it's time I want to give.

I wish I didn't have to keep any secrets from my brothers. I only have one secret, but if anything had the potential to get my ass tossed to the curb, fucking the club president's daughter would probably be the thing to do it.

"Keep it in your pants, ladies," Dog barks. "Prospect's not here to play."

I wink at Midge and take the cup of coffee she prepared for me. I nod my thanks to her before a grunt pulls my attention.

If I wasn't moving my ass before, I am now. Lia's dad, Tiny, a man whose name is the definition of irony, clamps a hand on my shoulder. "Move your ass, kid. You got shit to do," he says, no softness in his voice.

"I'm on it," I assure him.

I know the drill.

Normally, I'd have an hour of work to do around the club, but today, something else is up. Tiny texted me last night and told me to make sure I met up with him before I left the club to go to my job at the repair shop.

While I would have loved to spend another hour in bed with Lia this morning, time at the club is something I'd never give up. I've been spending at least an hour a day at the club, seven days a week. There's no set schedule or written-in-stone expectations for a prospect, but the goal of prospecting is simple.

Build trust.

Prove your loyalty.

Get to know your club brothers better than you know yourself.

Anticipate the needs of the club and fill them.

This morning, there's not a lot going on. Despite the early hour, Morris isn't in his room. The door is closed, and when I knock, there's no answer. I crack the door and see the bed is neatly made, so I close it back up again and head out to wash the bikes and assorted parked cars and trucks out back.

By the time I finish, it's nearly time to head over to the repair shop. Lia opens the strip mall for us in the morning.

Thinking of Lia, I grab my phone and shoot off a message.

Me: You make it out okay? Shop good?

I'm sure she's fine. Lia may seem like a hippie, but she's responsible and really hardworking. She opens the shop like clockwork and is sweet and professional. I just... It's been a couple hours, and as much as I love being in the compound, my mind keeps drifting to her body. To the waves of soft brown hair covering my face as I fuck her. The way she grunts, cries, and urges me on when I touch her.

My dick hardens as I think about our morning. Then my phone buzzes with a reply.

Lia: I made out great.

She punctuates the play on words with a bunch

21

of tongue-out emojis. I stifle a laugh and punch in a quick response.

Me: About to meet with your pops. See you soon.

I head toward Tiny's office, taking a few deep breaths and thinking unsexy thoughts to encourage my dick to knock it off. I get a reply from her and swipe to read it before I go in.

Lia: Give Tiny a big kiss for me.

I shake my head and jam my phone into my pocket as I knock on the door to the club office, three quick taps even though the door is open.

Dog is sitting in a chair across from an empty desk, leaning all the way back with a leg crossed over his knee. Whatever this meeting is about can't be too bad if Dog looks that relaxed.

"Dog." I nod at him. "Tiny coming?"

Dog nods. "On his way. He had to take a shit."

"Fuck you." Tiny's voice is loud and close behind me. He's carrying an enormous plastic cup with a straw in it.

I move out of the way so Tiny can cram past me and sit in the ergonomic office chair Midge got him last year.

"Come on," he says, so I follow him into the office and take the open seat across the desk from him, next to Dog.

"Morris comin'?" Dog asks.

Tiny shakes his head. "He'll be late. Kid business something or other. He texted."

"Zoey all right?" I ask.

Last year, when Morris got together with Alice, Lia and I spent a ton of time with Alice's kid, Zoey. She's a sweetheart and a real firecracker now that she's out from under the clutches of her shit-for-brains stepdad.

Tiny nods. "Yeah, it's nothing. Lice outbreak at school or something. Looks like Zoey brought the buggers home. The whole class got 'em. He and Alice had to stop by the school to sign some kind of form for her to be allowed back in class."

"Jesus… Kids." Dog shakes his head. "Who knew fucking lice was still a thing. Didn't we blot that shit out like we did with polio?"

Tiny coughs, a weird, raspy sound that makes me a little queasy. "Beats me, man," he says, chugging a huge sip from what looks like a half-gallon–sized pop cup. "My only contact with kids is with grown ones." He shoots me a look.

"No lice in our house," I say, trying to lighten the death stare Tiny's got aimed at me.

"Right," Tiny says, coughing again.

"You all right, man? That cough sounds…sick."

Dog tips his chin at Tiny, who waves a hand in the air dismissively.

Every time Tiny sees me, he finds a way to bring up his daughter. It's like he's got some father-radar and he knows we're fucking.

It shouldn't matter to him either way. Lia's a grown woman, for fuck's sake, and it's not like I'm some lowlife. Tiny only really got to know Lia a year ago when she found him after her mom retired and went off to live on some boat with her rich husband.

If I didn't know what it was like to have dead-beat parents and a brother who shot our only stability into his arm, I probably wouldn't begin to understand having kids you barely know. But the last year has taught me more tough lessons than I ever dreamed I'd have to learn.

Moral of the story? Everybody's family's got shit.

It's clear to me he doesn't like the fact that I live under the same roof with his daughter, no matter how "new" their father-daughter deal is.

I'm sure everyone does assume that we're fucking because we live together, but Lia tries to make it crystal clear we're not. To everyone, including me.

What we do behind closed doors, under the sheets and shit…ain't nobody's business. Especially not her dad's. But that doesn't mean I don't do my part to keep him from suspecting anything.

"Fucking hot wings," Tiny says, gulping down more soda. "Garlic pepper sauce is burning a hole in my throat."

"You ate that shit for breakfast?" Dog guffaws and shakes his head. "Jesus, man."

"All right, shut the fuck up," Tiny says. "We got shit to do, and we don't need to wait for Morris. This has to do with you," he says, his beady eyes boring into me.

Fuck.

"Fingers says we need cash." Tiny looks at me as though our cash flow is my problem.

Dog asks the obvious question. "Why's our lawyer involved? I thought the property we bought was straight. Insurance money and shit?"

Tiny shook his head. "Insurance money paid to rebuild the parts that burned, but inspectors found a shit-ton of code violations." He glared at me. "Your brother managed not only to drive the building into bankruptcy, but he greased the palms of a few city inspectors over the years. Hid the fact that underground storage tanks weren't handled properly, all kinds of amateur bullshit."

"The fact that my brother's a no-good douchebag is old news, Tiny," I say before he can say it. Every chance he gets, he loves to remind me that I come from nothing. It's almost as if he's afraid I'll forget. "Why is this a problem now?"

Tiny's beady eyes look me over. "We're finally ready to lease the space, but if we don't raise the rental prices and lock in at least a couple new tenants for two years, we'll be running in the red on the place for at least another five." He shakes his head. "Club can't sustain those kinds of losses that long."

"Fuck." Dog whistles between his teeth. "We bought that dump to turn it over fast and cheap."

"And if it hadn't been for that asshole ex of Alice's trying to burn it to the ground, we might have been able to get away with none of the defects coming out," Tiny says.

A sinking feeling hits me low in the belly. "You thinking about selling the place?" I ask.

Tiny shakes his head. "We can't. Once the fire damage was repaired, that shithole strip mall was about 65% new. An upgrade that size meant we needed to comply with all the codes in effect for new construction. Fingers worked some magic with the fire inspectors. Got us grandfathered in despite the reno and saved us five figures in mandatory upgrades to bring the property up to current code. But he made sure we knew that if we try to sell the place, they won't sign off on the sale unless we implement the upgrades."

"Goddamn," Dog says. "So, we're in the red on the reno, and if we want to sell and cut our losses, we've got to put another, what, fifteen to twenty grand into the place even to list it?"

"More than that," I say. I huff a frustrated sigh. My brother was a decent businessman before he became an addict, but he'd been an addict a long time. "Tim got estimates to install sprinklers in the place about four years ago, right before everything started going to shit for him. Back then, the price—even using some firefighter buddies who were licensed to do installs on the side... I think north of thirty G's, if I remember it right."

"Thirty grand?" Dog slaps his hands on his thighs. "Fuck. The club oughta prospect in somebody in construction. We could use that kinda cash."

Tiny shakes his head. "We're not putting in a

sprinkler, and we're not selling. That's why you're here," he says.

"Yeah," I say.

Whatever it is Tiny has in mind, I'm ready for it. I've cleaned toilets, done light carpentry, fixed bikes, boats, and trailers.

Shit, I even walked Midge's dogs when she gave herself food poisoning with one of those damn casseroles last year.

I'm ready to do something that can make a real impact on the club.

Tiny shoves some paperwork at me. "You know the building better than anyone," he says. "Your record is clean, and you're running an honest business. We need you to find somebody to rent that last space. We're raising the rent, and we need a two-year lockdown."

"Wait, I thought we needed two tenants. The nail salon's confirmed?" Dog asks.

Tiny nods. "We've gotta throw them some perks because we upped the rent from what we initially proposed, but we worked something out," he says.

I know what that means.

Kickbacks.

The nail salon is a match made in heaven, but that leaves one space to rent out.

"So…I'm looking for what?" I ask him. "It's not like I'm at church on Sundays having donuts or hosting community ice cream socials. I spend all my time with you assholes. What kind of business am I supposed to find to rent the space?"

Tiny glares at me. "Telling you what to do is my job, Prospect. How to get it done is your problem."

I sigh. Right. "How much time I got?"

"A month, tops," Tiny says.

"Anyone I can't rent to?" I ask. "Sex toy shop, adult film shoots, gun store?"

"If they have cash and sign for two years, I don't care if you film old ladies using flaming grenade dildos on each other while they smoke a bong," Tiny says. "We want a tenant who pays money. That's it."

"That's it," I echo. "Got it."

"Don't fuck this up," Tiny says and pushes back from the desk, grabbing his gallon of drinkable chemicals.

The threat is implied, but it's still there. I'm not a member of the MC yet, and nothing is guaranteed. If I want to earn my place in this brotherhood, I have a lot more ground to cover. And Tiny handed me a destination but didn't give me a map.

"I'm not my brother, man." I feel the need to

29

say it for the thousandth fucking time. "I'll get a tenant."

Tiny nods and wheezes his way out the door.

Once we're alone in the office, I go to stand, but Dog puts a hand on my shoulder to stop me.

"Hey," he says. "Speaking of...you heard from that brother of yours?"

I shake my head. "Not a peep. He could be dead or in prison for all I know." At this point, I didn't give a shit either.

"Tough." Dog nods as if he knows, has been there. Maybe he has. "Don't mind Tiny," he says. "You know the drill. Prospect bullshit. It's how it goes. And you living with his kid..."

I nod.

I know how it goes. I'm the asshole shacking up with Tiny's daughter.

I'm in his club, I'm in his daughter... Although thank fuck no one knows about that.

30

LIA

WHEN I ROLL into the parking lot at work, there is a truck parked right up front and a huge guy standing in front of Leo's repair shop. Ever since Alice's insane lunatic ex tried to burn this place down, we've had a really basic security system in place, motion-activated cameras that take still pics when something moves.

Alice and I both have panic buttons connected to the system too. Even though Alice's ex-husband is locked up for arson and assault, we work alone out here often enough that all the men in our lives —Morris, Tiny, Leo—feel better with us having panic buttons.

I finger mine, which dangles along with clear

pink plastic beads and cartoon character charms on my key chain as I turn off the car.

The truck is nice, big, but nothing special about it, and the guy looks harmless enough. He's sipping coffee from a thermal tumbler and checking his watch like he's waiting for the shop to open. I get out of my vintage VW van and leave the door open so Pixie, Violet, and Agnes can run out. They charge from the open back of the van toward the driver's side door, barking and panting up a storm.

"Morning!" I call out. "We're not open yet. Can I help you with something?"

The guy shoves a pair of dark sunglasses onto his head and nods. "Morning," he calls back. "You work here?"

I close the door to the van and lock it up while the girls run in mad circles up to the guy. They surround his ankles, and I grin, thankful the dogs have my back.

"Sure do," I call back. I flip my own sunglasses back and slow my pace as I approach the stranger.

He is hot. Like freaking, ovary-shattering hot. I can see that even from this distance. Even after a bone-melting orgasm this morning with Leo, I can't help noticing the thighs on this guy. Despite being hidden beneath his broken-in black jeans, his legs look like he could do squats for days.

"Need the auto repair shop?" I ask. "Cuz you don't exactly look like you're interested in doggie day care." The slightest hint of flirtation comes out in my voice. I can't help myself.

As I get closer, I can see the guy's got piercing eyes. Sort of a hazel-green combination, mostly brown but with a green-gray ring that attracts the light. He's clean-shaven, and his arms are covered in colorful tattoos from his wrists to the place where his biceps disappear under his black golf shirt. He's not only fit, but he's big—like, football player big.

"I'm actually looking for the guy who owns the shop," he says. "He around?"

"Oh," I say brightly. "Do you know Leo?"

He quirks a brow at me. "Hell yeah, I know Leo. But what about Tim? I thought Leo's older brother owned this place?"

The fact that he knows Tim's name makes me feel all right getting a little closer. He does know the Hawk brothers, so the fact that he's here at this hour and I'm all by myself seems a lot less worrisome.

"Hey, girls… Girls!" My dogs have stopped barking and running, but now they are swarming the guy's ankles, rolling on their backs in shameless bids for attention. Kind of like I imagine I might, now that I'm this close to the guy's bulging arms and twinkling eyes. "Sorry," I say. "My girl crew tends to be…social."

"Girl crew?" He looks down at my dogs and chuckles. "Never had a dog myself." He twists his lips into a grin that is pure heat. "But they suit you."

"Yeah?" I ask, picking up on a little bit of a vibe from him. "How so?"

"Pretty, playful…" He bends down and scratches Agnes's ear, and I know he's made the right call. He's got good instincts.

Agnes, despite being one of the two smaller dogs, is totally the alpha of the pack.

If he gets on her good side, the others will follow. That intrigues me about him.

He looks up at me as if he knows I'm assessing his personal worth based on the way he treats my dogs. "I'm Josh, by the way," he says, holding out a hand to me. "Josh Aronowicz."

I hold out my hand to him and shake his while he's still on bended knee. "I'm Lia Dove," I say. "Two first names. Mom was a total hippie, but you can call me Lia."

"Never would have guessed," he says around a

grin. "The VW van and your Coachella clothes kind of give it away." He releases my hand and stands. "Nice to meet you, Lia," he says. "You Leo's girlfriend?"

Wow, this one doesn't waste any time. I like his style.

I shake my head. "Roommate," I clarify. "I work over here in the doggie day care, and we live together—only as friends."

"Leo always was a lucky fucker," Josh says, a grin on his face.

"Well, thank you, handsome stranger," I say, upping the flirtation factor.

"So, this your girl crew?" he asks, standing up. Although it's clear Pixie is none too happy the petting is over.

I nod. "Part-time security detail and full-time family."

"I'm not usually a fan of dogs, but these ladies are pretty damn sweet."

"Why aren't you usually a fan of dogs?" That strikes me, of course.

I can't plant my hopes in a puppy-hater. Not that I'm planting hopes, exactly...more like stirring the pot a bit.

My eyes can't help tracing the broken-in denim

of his jeans. His tattoos alone are enough to send my body into overdrive. I'm blinking through the morning sunshine, trying to make out the designs while I drag my eyes away from those crystal-blue eyes. Most people love when you ask about their tattoos, but for some reason, I want to figure this guy out for myself.

"Occupational hazard," he explains. "I'm out on calls constantly. Run into a lot of people's dogs, and most, I can tell you, are not as friendly as your girl crew here."

"Well, they're good judges of character," I say. "And normally, so am I. You don't seem like someone we should be worried about."

Josh's lips curl into a smile, and it's sinfully sexy. Wicked with a dash of playful. "Who, me?" he teases. "You must be a good judge of character too if you can tell I'm innocent from only a few minutes of conversation."

"Now, innocence is something totally different," I say. It's getting late and I should open the shops, but this little banter we have going on is worth a few more minutes. I toss my hair over my shoulder and can't help noting Josh's reaction to the way my breasts bounce when I move. "You definitely don't strike me as the *innocent* type," I say.

As I'm waiting for his reply, Alice pulls up in her SUV and parks next to my van. I can see her checking out who I'm talking to with a look of interest, maybe concern.

I wave and she nods before she turns off the car and climbs out.

"Good morning," she says, addressing me and the sexy stranger.

"Good morning." Josh nods.

"This is a friend of Leo and Tim's," I explain. "He's looking for the owner of the building." I look at Josh with a question in my voice. We never got to why he was here. I got distracted by the volcanic eruption in my ovaries.

"My husband—fiancé—owns the place, and I manage it," Alice says. "Is there something I can help you with?"

Josh nods at Alice. "Just looking for Tim Hawk, actually. We were high school buddies."

Alice shakes her head. "I've actually never met him. But Leo should be here any time now. You should talk to him." She walks up and extends a hand to Josh, who shakes it, moving his travel mug to his left hand. Alice pulls the keys to the building from her laptop bag and unlocks her office. "You're welcome to come on in and wait."

I wouldn't mind a few more minutes with this hunk. "I'm right over there if you'd rather wait with the girls," I offer, pointing toward the day care.

"The Canine Crashpad?" he asks, a smirk on his lips.

Alice shoots me a look which I ignore. I know everyone suspects something's going on between Leo and me, but what we do have isn't anyone's concern.

"That's the one," I confirm. "Doggie day care and play place."

I can't help feeling like Alice is sending me some kind of warning with her eyes, a judgment maybe. She doesn't know anything about the arrangement I have with Leo, but still...she and I have had a little bit of that mom thing going on ever since I moved here.

Josh looks as if he's about to say something more when Alice disappears into her office.

Even though I'm not doing anything wrong, I can't help but feel like she thinks I am.

I don't see what the big deal is. There's no chance of the Leo thing being more than what it is —some shenanigans and sexy time. The roommate circle of trust. Some mutual scratching of an itch while we're under the same roof and conveniently single. Just because we've both stayed single the entire time we've lived together…

Well, shit. That doesn't mean anything.

Being a prospect of the club hasn't left Leo any time to have a social life or really to do anything that doesn't have to do with his club brothers, work, or me. And I've spent all my free time over the last year trying to get to know my dad again.

Growing up without Tiny was hard. But once my mom retired, I knew there was nothing holding me back. I got in my van, loaded up the pups, and left.

So here I am.

Living my life, getting to know my dad, building a business for myself in a new city, and having some no-strings-attached fun with Leo.

Just because Alice is engaged to Morris, happily coupled up raising her kid, doesn't mean that happily ever after is in the cards for Leo and me.

I'm young, he's young, and he is everything my father does not want for me. Even if I did feel more than lust for Leo, it would never, ever work.

That realization makes Josh look all the more interesting.

"So," I ask him, "you wanna come play with the pups while you wait?"

"THE PLACE LOOKS GREAT." Josh nods as he checks out my space.

"This is only primed," I tell him, pointing to the walls. "The walls needed some repair after the fire, and now that that's done, Alice's daughter is going to help me paint a mural."

"Fire?" He looks at me with concern.

"Yeah." I debate how much about the business I should share with him, but figure it can't hurt to tell him what happened. He's an old friend of Leo's, so I'm sure Leo will tell him all about it, if he hasn't already. "Alice, that lady you met outside, her ex-husband tried to burn the place down to get back at her for leaving him."

"Whoa." Josh's eyes widened in concern. "Shit, that sucks. Anyone hurt? What happened to the ex?"

I shake my head. "No. Thank goodness, no one was hurt, and the asshole is now serving out his days in a teeny tiny cell. Orange jumpsuit." I shudder. "Why the hell would anyone do something so stupid? Like, I get kids do dumb things, stealing lip gloss or candy from the drugstore, but trying to burn down a building?"

Josh doesn't seem to have any opinion about that. He walks the length of the space, bending down to look at the dog beds and bowls.

"Do the other businesses have any problems with you running a doggie day care right next door?" he asked. "I can imagine it gets pretty rowdy in here."

I laugh. "So far, so good. I only have a couple clients, and the building's been mostly vacant since the fire. We've got a nail salon that's supposed to move in, but we'll see, I guess." As proud as I am about the plans I've got for this place, it feels too personal to share with anyone at this point. Although, to be fair, I'm closer to Leo than any of them. He's the only one who knows all about the interview I have today.

Josh nods. "Did Tim flip his lid? I can't imagine how he reacted after the fire…"

I shrug. "I've never met Tim. Alice's fiancé owns the building, and I've been around for almost a year now and I've never met him." He meets my eyes, and I reach past him, playfully close, to pick up a stack of water bowls. "When was the last time you talked to Tim?"

"You've never met him?" Josh echoes. "But you

live with Leo? I feel like I've missed about a hundred steps."

He looks confused, concerned, almost. "I talked to Tim, like, what a couple weeks ago. He didn't mention any of this...not the building, not the fire."

I walk over to the utility sink and fill the dog bowls with cool water. "Well, all I know is Tim, I think, got himself into some bad business deals. I don't know, maybe he was dabbling in some drugs. Look, I don't know, and so I don't think it's right to speculate. The bank seized this place last year, and Alice's fiancé bought it. They kept Leo's repair shop as a tenant, repaired the damage with the insurance money, and now they're looking to rent out the other spaces."

Josh looks a little green.

"Hey," I say, walking up to him. I put a hand on his arm. "Are you all right?"

"Arrow?" The door opens, and Leo's voice echoes in the nearly empty space. "Holy shit, man!"

Arrow? I look to Josh, who's grinning at Leo.

"Look at you, little bro. It's been a minute." He walks up to Leo, and they give each other a man-hug that's half back-clap, half grunt. "I was catching up on things with Lia here."

When Josh says my name, something dark

crosses Leo's face. Something a little possessive, maybe?

The idea that he might be jealous of Josh talking to me gives me an odd thrill.

"Wait," I interrupt. I give Josh a cheeky look. "Who's Arrow? What is this, some kind of biker code?"

Now it's Josh's turn to look concerned. The sparkle in his eye and the easy grin he wore when Leo came in have all but faded.

"You in an MC now?" Josh nods at Leo.

Leo nods back, but I notice he's not wearing the vest with his prospect patch on it. "We've got a lot to catch up on, man." He looks at me and points to Josh. "Arrow's what we called him when we were kids. Aronowicz was a mouthful growing up."

"It's a mouthful still," Josh agrees.

If anything could have made Josh get a little bit hotter in my estimation, a nickname like Arrow would have done it.

"You keepin' your nose clean?" Josh asks, looking at Leo. "I know it's none of my business, but you were always the straight brother in the Hawk family."

"What? You mean with the club?" Leo scrubbed a hand over the back of his neck. "Hell yeah, man. It's legit. We only ride. None of that TV shit, running guns and crap. It's all good."

"Good. You were always the clean-cut one." Josh grins at Leo. "But your brother…remember that time he pulled that prank on Mr. Perrod in history class?" Josh turns to me. "Leo's brother Tim had a serious reputation for pranks," he explains. "Legendary. And it wasn't silly shit. Like, this dude made plans."

Leo looks happy too, like the memories of who his brother used to be when they were kids are good ones. He seems so much lighter, happier, talking about his brother. Memories he likes revisiting—unlike the recent ones, which seem pretty fucked up, if you ask me.

The dogs have started clawing at Leo's legs for attention. He shakes his head at them but bends down to scratch all three of the faces panting at him for love.

He's got this intense look on his face, and for some reason, my body goes back to this morning. To the way he looked at me as I was lying there naked. Teasing him. Taunting him. As if he didn't quite know whether to go hard or go soft. It's the same kind of expression I see now—as if the joy of

44

reminiscing about his brother is battling his buried rage over what Tim's done.

"So, what's the deal with the building, man? Tim didn't tell me anything about what's been going on here." Josh seems anxious to break the sudden tension, too.

"Wait. What?" Leo stands up, leaving the puppies wanting at his feet. The atmosphere in the room suddenly turns volcanic. "You've talked to Tim?" His shock turns to anger, and every emotion flickers across Leo's face. "Are you serious? When did you talk to him? Where the hell is he?"

Josh holds up his hands. "I mean, yeah, man. I talked to him a couple weeks ago. But he didn't mention anything about the fire or the building being bought."

Leo looks at me, and his face grows hard.

Oh fuck. All of a sudden, Leo looks like I've never seen him before. Angry, stunned. I don't know what.

"Leo," I interrupt, trying to smooth this over. "I told Josh about the fire. I was showing him around the place and catching him up on what we've been doing here."

Josh nods. "Lia mentioned you're trying to rent

45

some of the open stores here. I'm actually in the market for a new office. I was hoping I could check out the space, see what you're looking to get in rent."

Leo nods slowly, but it's clear his mind is still blown by the fact that somebody has heard from Tim. "Yeah? You're looking for a space?" He thinks for a minute. "Why don't you come by the house tonight for dinner? We can catch up on old times and talk about the business. What you do, what you're looking for in terms of space. I can have Alice show you the available unit now, but I need to head over to the shop and get it open. You remember where I live?"

Josh nods, but I can't tell why I'm sensing tension between them.

This feels a little different.

I'm not sure why Leo would invite Josh home instead of getting the full story here and now. That live wire sparks a bit more when Leo pulls his phone from his pocket and motions toward me. "Time, Lia. It's almost nine."

I scramble to dig my phone from my purse. Shit, he's right.

"I gotta hit the road anyway," Josh says, tugging his sunglasses back over his face and grabbing his coffee tumbler. "I can see the space another time. I'll see you at your place tonight."

He and Leo trade numbers. But everything has changed.

What started as a cool, fun reunion between old friends now has Leo's face a protective mask.

I watch the shifting dynamic play out between Josh and Leo as Josh heads toward the door and yanks on the handle.

"Hey, man," Leo adds. His eyes narrow as he squints at Josh. "Do me a favor. Why don't you invite my brother to dinner tonight?"

4

LEO

THAT MOTHERFUCKER.

I'VE SPENT the last year thinking my goddamn brother was dead. Terrified. Devastated. Worried until I was sick to my stomach. I had visions of my big brother dead in a ditch. In a flophouse someplace. Behind a dumpster, who the fuck knows.

Death was the only thing that could have kept the two of us apart, or so I fuckin' thought.

I'm not going to be able to focus on a thing. All I want to do is smash my fist through a wall or, better yet, through Tim's face.

Where the fuck has he been all this time?

My mind races as I open the shop. Just my luck, I have a ton of work to do. Starting with an electrical problem on a late nineties Cadillac. No one is around, and the routine of the job is probably the only thing that's gonna settle me down.

I pop the hood on the boat of a car and try to ignore the rage that makes me want to smash windows and take off on my bike. Run. It's what I want to do. But I'm not a chicken motherfucker who runs away from his problems. I'd run toward them. And right now, my brother has got a bull's-eye on his forehead.

All my hard work. *Our* hard work—my grandfather, my brother, and me. Our entire family legacy is tied up in this business, in this small, shitty strip mall.

How long has it been since I've seen my brother? Almost a year? Since I've actually had a phone call or a text? Proof of life, at least.

I can't fucking believe that in the last few weeks, Tim had been in touch with his friends, but not me. His flesh and blood. His younger brother. When he left, he left me with nothing. A business that was about to get taken by the bank. No way to earn a living.

No assets, no credit, no cash. *Nothing.*

If Morris hadn't kept me employed at the shop, I would have been out on the fucking street.

As much as I love my brother, I don't care what

he's snorted or shot up his arm. If Josh makes good on his promise to invite Tim to dinner, I'm gonna let that motherfucker have it.

Goddamn him!

My morning only gets worse as I run a diagnostic on this Caddy. Someone who didn't know what the hell they were doing tried to fix it before they brought it in to me.

Amateurs.

They always make it more expensive. My gramps used to love that phrase. He'd bust it out every time some cheap-ass came in, wanting him to "just" do this or do that to get a car running again.

You think hiring a pro is expensive? Try hiring an amateur.

My gramps's motto is the story of a mechanic's life. But today, this kind of bullshit is gonna fray my last nerve.

"Leo."

Lia's voice breaks me out of my funk.

I lift my face from the mess under the hood. "Yeah." I try to shake the rage from my voice as I meet her eyes.

She looks worried, but she's bouncing up and down on her toes, which I know means she's literally about to burst with excitement.

"Oh fuck," I say, "tell me. You had your call?" I look up at the old clock on the wall of the repair bay. It's almost ten. "What happened?"

She bounces through the shop and settles on the top of my grandfather's old metal desk. That thing has to be close to fifty years old. Knowing my granddad, he didn't buy it new. I watch as Lia settles her ample ass on the cool metal desktop. She's so excited, and now that she has my attention, I can see the outline of her nipples growing hard as she gestures her arms while she talks.

"It was so great," she says. "The program is one year long if I take it online, but if I come in and do what they call practical hours in the school's grooming bays, I can finish in closer to six months."

"Yeah?" I close the hood of the Cadillac, making a note that I'm going to need to call the owner and let them know it's probably gonna be another day before I even know what parts I need to undo whatever the hell they tried to do under here. "That's great."

I wish I could rally a little more enthusiasm. I hear how flat I sound about the whole thing, and I know how important this is to Lia.

"Yeah," she says. "It could be great. It's not cheap, Leo. Tiny said he'd pay for the whole program." She gives me a little, wistful smile. "The guilty dad card doesn't seem to have an expiration date. I didn't ask him to, but if I do the whole pet CPR certification and everything, the program's gonna be like five grand."

I nod. "That's okay," I say. "Let Tiny be a dad. He wants to do it, let him."

I can't help wondering if maybe that's part of the stress Tiny's feeling about money. Yeah, the club needs paying tenants in the strip mall, but as far as I know, Tiny has only ever worked for the MC. I have no idea where he'd get that kind of money, or if he has any money at all to help Lia.

This dog grooming certification is something she wants to do so badly. Seeing how happy it makes her talking about it takes a little bit of the edge off my rage.

"This could change everything for me, Leo," she says. "Not only a doggie daycare, but grooming and even some basic training. It could be the start of something really big. A franchise in the future if I get really successful. Canine Crashpad, coming to a city near you."

When she talks about it like that, she sweeps her arms wide. Her hair floats around her shoulders, and she looks like a sultry angel in short shorts. I'm proud of the way she's jumping into her dreams. Lia's really tight-lipped about her past, about her upbringing. She doesn't have much. Like me, I guess.

I have the MC and her. She has Tiny and me.

Thinking of it that way makes me want to be more supportive. The money shit is between her and her dad, but if my role is to help fill the space with a tenant and that can somehow ease the pressure on Tiny to pay for Lia's schooling, then that fixes it. I'm not going to let her down.

"So, what do you think?" I ask. "You goin' for it?"

Lia doesn't even hesitate a moment. She squeals and runs up to me. "Hell yeah, I'm gonna do it. Badass businesswoman, here I come."

She gives me a quick hug, holding her body firmly against mine. The touch is intimate, her hips pressing against mine, her tits flattening against my chest like they do when she lies on top of me in bed.

The moment is too real, too personal.

Too something.

I squeeze her back and release her quickly.

She knows our drill.

We don't show affection at work.

We don't touch each other away from what we do in private at home.

The sad look on her face reminds me that I'm not in a good place.

I'm overthinking this shit. I mean, if somebody walked in and saw me hugging my roommate, so fucking what? She has good news to share. And being a supportive roommate isn't the same thing as admitting to the world we're fuck buddies.

Even still, I can't keep holding her, or the steel in the front of my work pants is gonna give everything away. The last thing I need is Tiny or Alice walking into the shop while I'm sporting a hard-on for Lia.

She takes a minute before she pulls away. She lingers close to me, looking into my face. She's trying to read me. I know she is. I can smell the berry scent in her hair and the clean, fresh smell of some fruity lotion she uses on her skin. It's like I can never get away from her fragrance. It's in the bathroom we share at home. It's on her sheets. It's in her hair as she walks past me in the kitchen.

She's everywhere.

I close my eyes and breathe it in for a second, losing myself in how she makes me feel. It's the only good feeling—*Lia* is the only good feeling—I've had over the last year.

Even compared to the MC, which is important to me.

The MC means something to me, especially now that I know I can't count on my actual brother. I mean, fuck. I need a brotherhood now more than ever, but nothing makes me feel the way she does. Even if the feelings and what we do and how we do it are all wrapped up in a secret.

"Leo," she asks. "Are you okay? Be real with me."

I step back from her all-too-knowing look. "Yeah," I say. "You mean about Tim?"

She nods, a shadow crossing over her eyes. "I know we haven't talked about it much," she says. "But, honey, he's your brother. I can't imagine what you've had to deal with, not hearing from him all this time. With everything that's gone on with the business and now to find out that he's out there. He's talking to people…"

"He's not fucking talking to me," I fill in.

"Yeah," she agrees. "That. I'm so sorry, Leo. I can't imagine—"

I cut her off. "Don't worry 'bout it. Let's focus on you. You have good news, great things are ahead. Your dad's helping you out with school. You have a lot to be happy about, a lot to celebrate. And who knows? If Tim comes to dinner tonight, if Josh gets ahold of him like he said…"

"What are you thinking?" she asks. "Are you gonna kick his face in?" Lia is quiet for a moment. "What if Tim wants to move home?"

I hadn't thought about that. I mean, up until a few minutes ago, I'd pretty much been assuming my brother was dead. I don't know if alive and a total fucker is better than having him be gone forever. Dead. That's not a thought I wanna linger on too long.

"Don't worry about that," I reassure Lia. "Fuck him. He lost the right to live in that house a long time ago."

I feel strong as shit about that. Tim's not going to come back into my life after everything he's left me to deal with and kick out the one good thing I've managed to pull out of this shitshow—Lia.

"Leo, good to see you again, man." Josh grabs my hand and pumps it. He's got a backpack slung over one shoulder.

"Arrow." I hold open the door and wave him in. "Just one for dinner?"

I knew it.

I mean, I have to admit, I hoped…a small part of me hoped that Tim didn't show for dinner. I wasn't sure I wanted to see him, to take out the last year's emotions on him the way I knew I'd have to if he came through that door. But since he isn't here, I don't have to worry about what I might be tempted to do.

"Sorry, man," Josh says. He nods. "I texted him, but…"

I nod. He doesn't have to say any more. "Don't worry about it. Have a seat."

I lead Josh into the living room. It's fall, so I've got the windows of the house wide open. It's cool outside, and I have chicken marinating in the fridge.

"You want something to drink?" I ask. "I asked Lia to pick up more beer on her way home. She'll turn up in about an hour, and there's a chance she'll remember the beer. I've got a couple cold ones, though, if you're drinking?"

"I'm all right, man." He looks uncomfortable. He hasn't sat down, and he's looking around the house like he's not really in the mood to be here.

57

I jerk my chin at him. "What's up? Something on your mind?"

He sets down the backpack and starts unzipping it. "I'm not planning on staying for dinner, Leo. This is a business call."

"Business?" I drop down onto the couch and motion for him to sit. "We talkin' about the office space?"

Arrow shakes his head. "'Fraid not, man."

"I'm not following."

"I'm here as a courtesy," Arrow says. "I feel really bad for you, Leo. I want you to know none of this is personal."

I'm not sure where this is going, but when he pulls a manila folder out of his backpack, my blood starts running ice-cold.

"What's that?" I ask.

He holds the folder out for me to take.

I grab it and flip it open, starting to look through a stack of paperwork. I see a lot of names and information I recognize—and a whole lot of shit I don't understand. "Fuck me. This is about Tim…" I'm finally piecing it together.

He nods. "Leo, again, man, if I'd had any idea about everything going on… Well, this shit would have gone down different. Tim called me a while back. He was in trouble, arrested."

That explains a lot.

That asshole was in jail this whole time? But Arrow is sounding like this is the beginning of a story I am not going to like the ending to.

"He got himself into a lot of trouble, Leo. Serious shit. Seems like your brother was caught up in a small-time drug operation. He was dealing some new drug college kids are going crazy for. Tim got pinched. That's when he called me."

I finger the business card stapled to the inside of the file folder.

Joshua Aronowicz

Licensed Florida Bail Agent

Holy fuck.

"All right. I know my brother's a junkie. I didn't know he was in business, though." I'm looking through the paperwork, and I'm reading it. But I can't fucking believe what I'm seeing. "So, what does all this mean? What does this have to do with you?" I ask.

Arrow rubs his forehead, grimacing. "I need to find your brother, Leo. *You* need to find your brother."

I can hardly make out what Josh is saying. He's

saying the words and he's explaining, but the blood rushes in my ears, making them ring, and it's like I hear every other word.

"Tim called me. He couldn't post bail. He put up the house as collateral."

That's the only word I need to hear to completely understand the gravity of the situation.

Collateral.

That's how this all came down on my doorstep.

That's why Arrow showed up at the shop this morning. My brother gave Josh—not his old high school buddy Arrow, but fucking bail agent Josh Aronowicz—a call when he got arrested and couldn't make bail. And he used the deed to our house as a get out of jail free card. He put up the house as collateral.

"So, what…what happens now?" I ask. "Are you here to take my fucking house?" I ask the question, but my fists are clenched. I'm not about to be put out of my own goddamn home. The only thing I have left in this world. Not without a fight.

Josh holds out his hands. "No, Leo. Calm down, man. We're not there. Not yet. Let me explain."

I try to listen as Josh tells me what's happened over the last few months.

No wonder I haven't heard from fuckin' Tim.

He got pinched and put the house up as collateral against $150,000 bail. A hundred and fifty K. I literally can't believe what I'm hearing. Last I checked, our house was worth one-seventy, tops.

"Do you take the whole house?" I demand. "What if it's worth more than the bail?"

Arrow shakes his head. "Won't matter. When the house is put up as collateral, part of the deal isn't to protect the accused's assets. You won't get a dollar-for-dollar refund if the house is worth more than Tim owes. If he doesn't show up to court and I seize the house, you'll get nothing."

God fucking damn my brother.

"Why'd he call you?" I ask. "How did he even know to call you?"

"Occupational hazard," Arrow admits. "Most of us who are good at what we do, it's not hard to find us. I'm sure when Tim got arrested, all he had to do was have his wife ask around. Bars, even the jails. You name it. The only place you'll never find me is social media."

He tries to crack a joke, but it ain't gonna land. I'm still tripping on something he said.

"Wife?" What in the actual fuck? "Man, Tim's not married. Or at least, he wasn't."

Just when I stopped feeling like I needed to

smash Tim's face in, I wanted to smash Arrow's face in. Now, I'm back to wanting to kill my brother again.

"The marriage is legit, man, or at least as legit as a courthouse deal gets." Josh shakes his head. "I think she's his mule, honestly. I think he probably married her so she couldn't testify against him. She's the one who found me while Tim was locked up. But listen, Leo."

I lift my chin and grip the folder of paperwork in shaking fists.

"There's still a chance to save your house."

He makes it sound like a good thing. Like there's any reason to feel hopeful in this mess.

"Part of the deal when you work with a bail agent is doing whatever they require. Tim was supposed to check in with me twice a week, every single week, until the trial. When I didn't hear from him Friday afternoon like I was supposed to, I called. Then I texted. But when he didn't respond, that's when I showed up at the building."

"Wait…" I look Josh over. "If Tim put up the house, why did you come to the strip mall? Why didn't you come here first?"

"Well, I didn't know he didn't own the place

anymore. He told me you guys still had the shop and were working together."

That trips my interest. Tim had to know the building was about to be seized when he ran off a year ago. Why else would he have left? He may have been dealing drugs and on the run from me, but if he didn't put up the building, he had to know that it wasn't his anymore to stake against his bail.

If he offered up the house, that meant he also had to know I was still here. And the way Josh explained it, it sounds like Tim might know I am still working at the shop. Unless telling Arrow we were both still working at the shop was an outright lie?

It grates the shit out of me that this guy I haven't seen since high school knows more about my brother and his business than I do.

Josh looks apologetic. "I figured if he was still working, he'd be at work. That was my first stop."

"What if you hadn't found me there? Then what?" I don't think I want to know, but I have to ask.

"Look, Leo. If I'd found Tim at the shop this morning, I would have checked in with him and reminded him of his duties until that court date. That would have been the last of it."

63

"Right," I grit out. "But he wasn't there."

Arrow nods. "This isn't the first time someone lied to me to protect someone they love from the consequences of their actions."

"What are you talking about?" I stifle the urge to kick this asshole out of my house—while it still is mine.

"Tim has to know that when he didn't check in, I'd come looking for him." Arrow shrugs. "He's either sniffing around and will show up at some point, or he's in the wind for good now."

Fucking great.

"If he's sniffing around, I think I'd know about it," I said.

Arrow shrugs. "Maybe. Maybe you would but wouldn't feel right telling his bail agent about it."

"Are you fucking kidding me, man? You think I'm hiding Tim from you?"

Arrow doesn't say anything, but he looks me in the eyes, a challenge there.

"I'm not gonna lie. I'm trying really hard not to bounce your ass out of my house," I say. "But I'm acting civil because you've got the information I need. If you hadn't shown up tonight, I might never even know that he'd put up the house. After what I've been through this last year, you can bet your ass, if I see my brother, you'll be the first call I make."

Correction. The second.

The first call would be for an ambulance. Somebody's gonna need to stop the bleeding when I punch my brother in the face.

"Look, Leo, I get that you're hot right now, but there's still a way to save the house." He explains how the collateral against the bail bond works.

It all makes sense to me, what Josh is saying, where he's coming from. But there's a problem.

"Tim knows that if he doesn't check in with you, you'll come looking for him. Yeah?"

Arrow nods. "And I have the right to haul his ass back to jail where he'll rot until the trial." He looks at me. "I don't think Tim wants that, man. He knows he's got a court date coming up in two weeks. Between now and then, I need to find your brother. If I don't, and if he doesn't show for the pretrial hearing…"

Arrow looks around my living room and back at his boots.

I get it.

"Can you give me the name of his wife? Have you tried calling her?" I ask. There's got to be a way to get out from under this.

Arrow shook his head. "Privacy reasons, I can't say much, but the information is available online if you know where to look. I tried calling her when I couldn't teach him." He shook his head. "Burner phone, no doubt. When I called the number she used to call me, it was dead. Not in service."

My stomach sinks even lower, hearing that.

Arrow pretends to look at an imaginary watch on his wrist. "I can't tell you anything confidential, but if I told you a tiny blond girl named Juliette likes to hang out and shoot pool at Checkers on South Fairfax Avenue... And that she might know where to find your brother..." He looks at me again. "You wouldn't know enough about Tim's wife to track her down, but you could probably get a lead on her. You feel me?"

I want to feel Arrow. I want to feel his nose crunch under my fist. But I have to appreciate the guy is doing what he can here. He is trying to stop my brother from stealing the only goddamn thing I have left right out from under me. While at the same time saving his own ass on this bond. I have the feeling that getting Tim was a much better deal for Arrow than getting our house would be.

"I feel you," I grit out, clenching my hands into fists so hard my knuckles pop.

"We have two weeks until the court date. Your brother needs to be on time, at the courthouse, and in his seat for that hearing. It's the only way to save your house." Arrow stands and gives me a curt nod. "I know it doesn't feel like it, but we're actually on the same side here, Leo."

"Right." I slap the folder closed and drop it onto the coffee table. "I'd say thank you for letting me know, but don't hold it against me if I'm not exactly feeling grateful."

Josh shrugs but has the decency to not look around or look back at me. He lets himself out.

I lean my head in my hands before letting out a slow breath. "Goddamn you, Tim."

Not even ten minutes later, the door opens.

"I'm home," Lia sings out as she comes through the door. "Leo. Are you okay?"

"Come here, Pixie." I scratch the ears of the little bugger, and she frantically licks my hand as if I dipped it in a vat of bacon. I'm feeling a little better seeing her floppy ears and happy tail. A *little* better.

Lia's carrying a twenty-four pack of beer, and it looks as if the cardboard is about to slip out of her hands.

"Jesus, let me help you with that." I jump up

67

and leave Pixie and grab the cardboard box from Lia's hands.

"Sorry I'm late," she says. "I know you gave me one thing to do, but I got distracted."

I shake my head, but I'm not mad. That's why I had Lia pick up something that wasn't necessary to actually making the meal. I knew she'd be an hour late, at least, as she always is. But she's here now. She got the beer, and she's looking gorgeous. Too bad dinner's canceled and I have shit news.

"Dinner's not happening," I tell her.

"Wait...why?" She sits beside me on the couch. "You look like shit, babe. What happened?"

Lia takes my face in her hands. She smooths the scruff of my beard with her fingertips, stroking the line of my jaw and trailing her way down my neck. I love when she does that to me. It's my kryptonite. I close my eyes and tell her everything. She listens intently, looking scared at first, and then sad. Finally, her eyes fill with resolve.

"We have two weeks?"

I nod.

Lia looks at me with something I don't recognize in her eyes. It's serious and yet so, so caring. She nods and takes my hands in hers. "Well, let's do it. Let's find your brother."

5

LIA

"LEO, COME ON. LET'S GO." I pound on the door of the bathroom.

As soon as I heard that Tim's wife liked to hang out at Checkers, I knew we had to go. Leo left the food he'd planned to make for the failed dinner with Josh in the fridge, and I changed my outfit into something more appropriate for hitting the seedy club.

Checkers isn't a place I've been to a lot since moving to Florida. I drove right past it probably a million times, thinking it was probably as dirty and scary inside as it looked on the outside, until one night I realized they had a darts league. We were bored, and I figured it would be cool to check it out.

Leo humored me by tagging along. The place definitely has the vibe of a closed club. Quiet conversation, dark lighting. The least chatty bartenders you'll ever meet. But if Juliette hangs out there, we at least have to try to find her there.

Leo opens the bathroom door and pushes past me. "This is pointless, Lia," he says, sounding annoyed. "I don't know what we're expecting to find at this fucking place. Tim hanging out at a table, tossing back beers with friends?" He shakes his head.

"We have to try," I remind him. "We have two weeks to find Tim, so we start with what we know. We check out this bar, ask if anyone knows Juliette or has seen Tim. If we don't get anywhere, we go on to the next thing."

Leo slips on his leather vest, the one with his prospect patch. "What's the next thing, Lia? Tim hasn't contacted me in a year. He hasn't wanted to be found. And now? With a criminal trial ahead and a bail agent after him? This is a big waste of time."

I stand in front of him and grab his shoulders. I look into his eyes and give him a shake. "Leo, I know this sucks. I know how shitty it feels that the one person you love and trust in the world can take everything from you and not even seem to care."

The words flow out of me before I realize how close to home they hit. I'm growing emotional for Leo, but truthfully, for myself as well. I blink away the tears and I try to rally my anger, because if that's what we need to save Leo's house, my home, that's what I'm going to do.

"It's not the first goddamn time, Lia." He looks really angry now, but I know he's not directing it at me. "Do you know what it was like to have to steal back my own shit from the building when Morris bought it? To watch the only job I ever had disappear because Tim threw it all away?"

He rubs his face with his hands, and I catch a whiff of his cologne. I want to hold him close and ease the pain he's feeling. We're not that different, Leo and I. He lost the only family he ever had way too young, way too painfully. I grew up without a dad and basically raised myself while my mother worked. Different paths to the same outcome.

"Don't think about that tonight," I urge. "Let's just check out this club. It's one thing we *can* do. We still have some control over what happens."

"We don't even know what Juliette looks like.

71

How will we know her if she's there?" Leo's softer now, sounding resigned.

"That doesn't matter," I tell him. "I have a plan. We need to get there and start acting like the kind of people Juliette will want to find her."

Leo tilts his chin at me and gives me a smoldering look. "You look amazing," he says. "Fuck this. Let's stay home and have a satisfying night in. Drowning my sorrows in you sounds like a much better way to spend my time."

I'm tempted. Jesus, I'm tempted.

It doesn't matter if we got it on this morning or an hour ago—Leo does something to me. Looking at him in his broken-in jeans and the skintight T-shirt with his vest on, I feel my mouth practically water. His shoulders are sagging under the weight of what's going on, but I know every muscle and ridge in his body. I can picture the freckles and spots on his skin, the tiny scars and every bit of ink that makes him my Leo.

I hate seeing him this way. It does something. Not only to my body, but to my heart.

I squeeze his shoulders under my hands and tug him close.

"We still have a house to come back to," I

remind him. "There will be plenty of time for *satis-faction*..." I try to press a light kiss against his lips, but Leo returns the kiss by crushing me against the hallway wall.

I close my eyes and kiss him back, losing myself in the feel of his hands in my hair. He tugs hard, harder than normal, but the tiny prickle in my scalp sets my whole body on fire. It's like that line between pleasure and pain is so thin, but Leo walks it like a pro. When he drags his mouth from mine, he doesn't take his hands from my hair, but he pulls my head back to look at me.

"I'm sorry to drag you into this," he says. "Something about it doesn't feel right. My family's shit... Maybe you should go live with Alice and Morris, at least temporarily. I'll see if there's a room I can crash in at the club..."

"Leo!"

Now it's my turn to tug on him. I pull away from his hold and grab his hands. "Listen to me," I demand. "We have options if it comes to that, okay? Neither one of us is going to be out on the street if Josh takes the house. But for two more weeks, *this* is our home. We're in this together, okay? And I'm not giving all of this up without a fight."

"All of this?" he echoes.

I nod. "We're best friends," I remind him. I almost start to say something else, but there's more bubbling under the surface than Leo's anger. I don't want to overcomplicate this. Things are complicated enough.

I think Leo feels the same way.

He nods. "Yeah…" He releases my hands and shakes his head. "You're right. I guess. It's only one night."

He smooths his T-shirt and runs a hand through his hair.

"All right, here goes nothing. You ready?"

"Yeah…" I tap the vest on his chest. "Let's go catch your brother's wife." I turn to head downstairs, but Leo stops. He heads back to his bedroom, shrugging off his leather vest as he goes.

"This isn't a night I want associated with the MC. Having anything that could identify me or the club later…" He looks a little torn, like he is having to choose between two parents. In a way, he is choosing between two families. But only for a temporary goal.

"Good call," I say. "Besides, we should take your truck, not the bike. Maybe we'll have fun and have a drink or two. I want to be able to drive us home if you get rowdy."

I nudge him playfully, and he nudges me back, the shadow of my Leo coming back to me. We head downstairs, and I give a few kisses to the dogs. Leo locks up the house, and we climb into his pickup. We make the drive to Checkers in silence, and when we get there, he parks at the back of the parking lot, between two other trucks, far from the door.

"If Tim is here," he explains, "he'll recognize my truck."

I nod, and we head across the parking lot. I step close to him and grab his hand. He flicks a questioning look at me. We never hold hands in public, display affection of any kind. "Cover story?" I ask, smirking at him. "In fact, maybe we should use fake names…"

Leo squeezes my hand before he releases it. His expression darkens.

"What is it?" I ask, following his eyes.

"Arrow's truck," he says, jerking his chin toward a sleek black pickup. I don't remember enough about Josh's truck from earlier to be sure that's him.

"You sure?" I ask. "I didn't really pay attention to it this morning." I didn't add that I was too fixated on the guy himself. And his tattoos. And the beefy muscles underneath those tatts.

"Not one hundred percent," Leo admits. "But it would make sense he'd be here too."

I hadn't thought about that, but, yes, it does make sense. If we are staking out Tim, odds are good that Josh would too. Especially since he didn't find Tim where he expected to—at the shop or the house.

"Should we use fake names or something?" I ask him. "What if we—"

Leo grabs the door to the bar. "Let's play it by ear. If Arrow's here, we're not going to be able to keep a cover story in place." He holds the door open for me. "Go on. Stay close to me and be careful. If anything seems off, we bail."

As we head inside the dark bar, I shove past him and give my ass a little shake to remind him to lighten up a little. He looks like he's here for a fight, and I may not know Checkers, but any time a man walks into a bar looking like Leo does, with an expression like that on his face—losing his house would be only one of many problems Leo was inviting in.

Checkers is exactly as I remember it. Scarred tables with rickety chairs are scattered throughout the poorly lit space. Neon signs on the walls are promoting beer brands, but most of them have stopped working or have been damaged. I can't help wondering if there have been brawls in here. Maybe flying beer bottles, or even heads, cracked the signs. But the drug-den décor doesn't seem to put a damper on the people in the place.

Every table is full. There's a rowdy game of darts being played, and the bartenders—a woman and a man—are slinging drinks to a packed bar. I can see Leo scanning the crowd, looking for Tim or maybe Josh. I'm not sure. I'm not sure what he'll do if he sees either of them.

I feel the heat of his hand against my lower back. "Let's get a drink." He nods at me, urging me to make my way through the crowd.

We stand as close as we can get to the bar—which isn't close at all. The male bartender looks us over, his face a sullen mask. I can see from this distance he has unusual scars on his right hand. Old, well-healed, but big.

Leo nods at the man, who nods back. Leo asks for a beer and holds up two fingers. He pays for the drinks and steers me away from the bar. I can feel the eyes of the people in the crowd burning into my back. We must look out of place, especially with me in my fringed white boho top and short shorts.

It suddenly occurs to me that we must stick out like sore thumbs. I can't believe that I thought this would be a good idea. "We probably shouldn't stay too long," I say. "Do you see your brother?"

Leo shakes his head no. "Drink your beer. I'm going to hit the head." He motions toward the back of the bar. "I wanna walk the place, act like I'm looking for the can, and see if there's anyone in there, anything that I can connect to Tim. If not, let's get the fuck out of here."

I nod, not letting on to Leo that I'm nervous he's going to leave me alone. I take a sip of my beer and avoid looking at anyone in particular. I play it cool and try to blend in with the crowd of people all dressed in drab and dark clothes.

Checkers does one thing right. The beer is ice-cold, and the bubbles hit my tongue just right. I drink it down and try to act casual. I don't look around and attempt to behave like I would any other time I was alone at a club. I focus on my beer and make an effort not to make eye contact with anyone.

"Come here often?" A voice behind me causes

me to twirl. When I meet the familiar gray-green eyes, I frown.

"No," I say. "But why am I not surprised that I'm running into you here?"

Josh looks at me with something akin to shock on his face. "Hey," he says. "I'm sorry about what's going on. It's not personal."

Not personal? "Try telling that to someone who's about to lose the roof over their head." I'm pissed at the guy for what's happening, but deep down, I can't hate him.

It's not his fault, any more than any of this is Leo's fault. He's doing his job. Tim's the one we should all be mad at, and still...

"I shouldn't be fraternizing with the enemy." I turn to walk away, but Josh stops me with a hand.

"Enemy?" he echoes. He looks disappointed, but his face quickly hardens. "Look, I don't know what Leo told you, but you shouldn't be here." He flicks a look toward the bar. "This whole place. Nothing but eyes and ears."

"Really?" I demand. "But funny how none of those eyes and ears seem to know where Tim is."

Josh glances over at me and, for a moment, looks like he wants to curse me out, but he doesn't. He doesn't speak at all.

"All right," he says finally. "I get it, okay? You're pissed and I get it, but you need to get your boyfriend and get out of here. This place isn't safe."

"He's not my boyfriend," I snap, without even thinking about it. I'm pissed off now. This guy is the one who holds our future—my future—in his hands. And he's telling me to shut up and go home? "And apparently, home isn't safe anymore either."

I turn away, ready to go hunt down Leo, when I feel a hand on my arm. A zing of heat travels along my skin, and I melt, just a little. I'm not here for that, though. Josh may be sexy and dangerous, but he's the reason Leo and I may lose our home. I can't afford to entertain even a little bit of lust for him, no matter how his touch makes me feel.

"Lia." Josh's voice is low, like he doesn't want anyone else to hear him talking to me. "Dance with me."

"What?" I squint at him. There are a few women tapping the necks of the beer bottles together, swaying to a country rock song, but no couples are dancing.

"Come on. Privacy."

He holds out his hand, and I grudgingly set down my beer on a table already cluttered with empty glasses and take his hand. The next thing I know, he's tugged me close.

I reluctantly slide my hands around his back and rest them on the freakishly toned muscles of his lower back. He shakes his head and unlaces my hands. He moves them to his shoulders and secures his arms behind my back. Our hips bump together as we barely sway with the song. My breasts rub against his chest, sending sparks flying through my middle.

Damn, why does the one man I hate have to be so hot?

Josh lowers his head and whispers against my hair.

"You shouldn't be here. If Leo wanted to come looking for his brother, that's on him. This is no place for you."

"I didn't give him a choice," I snark back.

I try to focus on the anger I'm feeling at Josh because with him this close to me, with his enormous arms around me, my body is being a traitorous bitch.

My knees grow weak, and I want to close my eyes, rest my head against Josh's chest. But I can't. This is only physical. He's a hot piece of ass, emphasis on the ass. I can't want him. He's not a good guy.

I tug my arms free and step away from him as Leo comes up beside me.

"You two having fun?" Leo asks. It's clear he's not amused.

He doesn't greet Josh at all, and Josh responds in kind, maybe realizing it's better that they don't appear as if they know each other.

"You plannin' on going home?" Josh asks, his voice icier now. He looks at a watch on his wrist. "It's getting late."

"We just got here, so we're good." Leo turns away abruptly and takes my elbow.

He leads me to a corner where the crowd is a little thinner. There are no open tables or chairs, so we stand together, my back to the crowd.

"I can't believe that guy," I say. "I don't like the game he's playing. Even though this is his business, this is our lives. Does he have any compassion? Any heart at all?"

Leo is quiet, scanning the crowd and sipping his beer. If he's thinking anything about catching me in Josh's arms, he sure as hell doesn't say anything about it, which almost makes me feel worse.

"I wanna get you out of here," he says. "I don't

know what the fuck we thought we were gonna accomplish. I don't think this is safe."

"What? Leave now?" I ask. "We just got here."

I have an idea.

"I think a cover story makes a lot of sense." I give him a light shove and shake my head. Then I raise my voice. "Can you fuck off? We're room-mates, okay? I'm not your girlfriend. I'm allowed to talk to whoever I want."

I give him a look and turn away, heading back toward the bar. Sweet-talking my way into and out of anything is something I used to be able to do. It wasn't something I'd had to do since I met Leo. But it's time to see if I've still got it.

I head over to the bar. There's not an open seat anywhere, so I rest a hand lightly on the shoulder of a burly dude in a black T-shirt. "Mind if I slip past?" I gesture toward the table where I set down my empty beer. "I could really use a refill."

The guy looks behind him as if he's checking to see if I'm alone or with anyone. "Yeah," he mutters, not looking too interested in talking.

"Thank you." I turn on the charm and give him a smile. The guy's older, gotta be nearing fifty. But guys my dad's age always seem to love chatting me up at bars, so I trust this bruiser's no different.

I stand patiently between the big guy and the man next to him, waiting to catch the bartender's eye. But I'm not trying too hard. I scratch my nail against the top of the bar, staring at the taps, trying to decide what else might be good. Basically doing everything I can to act cool, and finally, I think it works.

"You here alone?" the burly guy asks.

Bingo.

"Roommate's back there somewhere." I motion toward the crowded room without looking back. "But we're not here together, if that's what you're asking." I give him a guarded smile. The kind that's friendly, polite, but not over the top. I don't want him to think I'm playing him for drinks or coming on too strong. I stare down the bar and make safe, polite conversation.

"I've never been here on a weeknight before," I admit.

That's another thing I learned in the year I spent on the road. Before I found a place to stay with Leo, I spent a whole year living out of my van with my pups. I learned a lot about people—for better or worse. Men especially.

"I thought they had a decent dart game, but I might be thinking of the wrong place."

The guy on the barstool sizes me up. "Darts are over there," he says, using his beer bottle to point to the games. "But they're pretty closed up. Not a lot of space for newcomers."

"I get it," I say. I shrug and toss my hair over my shoulders. Getting it off my chest will give the guy an unobstructed view of my cleavage. "Maybe I should roll. A girl could die of thirst trying to get a beer." I move like I'm going to leave, like I'm getting impatient. I don't look at the man, but I stare off at the bartenders as if getting another drink or deciding to leave is my only focus.

The guy beside me nods. "Pat," he calls out. "Another round—and one for the young lady."

The bartender looks at us both and nods.

"Thank you," I say to the man. I offer him my hand. "I'm Lia."

"Nice to meet you, Lia," he says. I notice right away he doesn't give me his name, but at the same time, he gets up off his barstool and nods. "You wanna have a seat?"

OVER THE NEXT HOUR, I talk to my bar buddy. I still don't know his name, but that doesn't matter.

He's asking me a lot of questions, easy things I can answer. I can tell he's feeling me out. He's asking things like where I grew up, what I do.

I get the sense he's either trying to figure out whether I'm interested in him or if I'm a cop or something—maybe both. And that's interesting information. Whether it's useful or not, I'll find out eventually.

When he finally gets around to asking what I do, my answer seems to interest him. "I own a doggie day care," I say. "Nothing fancy. I get to do what I love without feeling like I punch that nine to five."

"You a dog lover?" he asks. But something in the way he asks makes me think he's still digging for information.

"I am," I say. This is no time to not be honest. I don't know who this guy is or what, if anything, he may know about Juliette and Tim. But the fact that he was able to get me a beer and that a bunch of people shifted seats to make room for him when he gave up his stool for me makes me think he's at least part of the regular crowd here. "Animals are a good business," I say.

Something in his demeanor changes. I'm not

sure what I said or didn't say, but it's clear he's done talking.

"Well, Lia." He stands and gives me a pleasant nod. "Maybe I'll see you around here again some time."

"I'd like that," I say. I can't thank him by name because he never gave it to me. I am pretty sure that was intentional. "Thanks for the beer."

I watch him walk away and notice he and the bartender trade a look as he goes.

Leo is behind me before anyone else can grab the empty seat. "You really know how to make friends," he growls.

I shrug. "Depends on your idea of a friend."

"Let's go," he says. He lowers his voice. "We're getting the fuck out of here."

I nod and leave my empty beer bottle on the bar. I don't see Josh anywhere until we're near the door. I see him, sitting at a crowded table. He's got his back to the wall, and a woman in black jeans and a black denim jacket is sitting on his lap. He doesn't make eye contact with us. Whether it's intentional or not, it's probably for the best.

We walk through the crowd and head for Leo's truck. We don't speak, and I'm too caught up in trying to think through my conversation with the man at the bar. Nothing. I come up with absolutely nothing. It's not like I had any natural openings to ask if he knew a woman named Juliette. And I'm guessing from the tightness in Leo's face, he didn't learn anything helpful either.

Once Leo pulls away from the parking lot, he seems to breathe a lot easier. "That was fucking pointless. And I was worried sick the whole goddamn time you were talking to that guy." He sniffs hard and looks over at me. "I couldn't even talk to anyone. All I did was stare at you two. All I could picture was him slipping something into your drink and carrying your ass out of there."

That honestly had never occurred to me. That I could be in some sort of danger like that. I was worried about finding Tim's junkie wife, not about the guy who practically acted like he was forced to talk to me at the bar. While it's sweet that Leo cares, I'm a little surprised he watched me the whole time.

"Did you find out anything?" I ask. "Talk to anyone?"

He grunts, and I take that as a no. "What about you?"

I shake my head. "No. Nothing at all. The only thing I know is the guy I was talking to never told me his name. Most guys aren't like that. They want your number, and they come on strong. Maybe it's the place, maybe it's me, but nothing really came of it. I don't even know what I was hoping for," I say.

It all kind of starts to hit me now.

"I'm so sorry, Leo. This was a stupid idea. Playing undercover cop or whatever. I don't know what I was thinking. It seemed like the only thing we could do."

Leo doesn't say anything, only stares straight ahead while he drives.

"Who was that woman wrapped around Josh?" I ask.

Leo looks at me, a slow stare that drags his attention away from the road. "Not Juliette," he says. "And not his girlfriend. Some barfly. I don't know. Somebody who's sent him business in the past, no doubt." His voice changes as he tells me, "Arrow stared you down almost the whole time you were talking to that guy. He's into you, Lia."

He says it like an accusation.

"Me?" I ask. "Weird."

"Right." Leo's voice is hard now. "It's so weird that a guy would be attracted to you, Lia. Into you. It's not like I didn't see the two of you dancing. You looked pretty damn into him too."

"Wait a fucking minute." I turn in my seat to

face him. "We went to that bar to try to find your deadbeat brother's wife, so we could maybe find a way to save your house. And you're going to give me a hard time because I danced with your brother's bail agent for like thirty seconds? You realize all he said to me was that we should go home?"

I refuse to talk to Leo the whole rest of the ride. I was right earlier. There's nothing shittier than being hurt by the people you love and trust most in the world.

6

LEO

"Lia... Lia, wait up."

I follow Lia into the house, but she's moving at warp speed. Goddamn, when she gets mad, she gets mad.

"Lia!"

I lock up the garage and the truck and let myself into the house. Lia's already in the backyard, letting the dogs out.

I head out back and grab a lawn chair. I drop down into the seat and stare up at the stars. Lia is walking through the grass barefoot. She's kicked off her shoes, and when she bends over to pet the dogs, the curve of her ass cheeks peek out of the bottom of her shorts.

I look away from her and stare at the backyard

of the only home I've lived in since I was five years old. The memories keep coming back to me. Tim and me after we lost our parents. Moving in with my grandparents. Learning about engines and cars and boats—anything that moved—from my grandfather.

How and why Tim went astray…I don't know. Who the fuck knows how my prank-loving, life-of-the-party older brother got hooked on drugs? Maybe he always had problems. I don't know. Seems like as soon as Gramps was gone, Tim started acting erratically, racking up debt against the business. That's probably when he got into drugs, but I don't know the details. Probably never will unless we find him.

My brother and I were close growing up, but people change. They go through their own shit. I don't know if I ever really knew what he was struggling with, how things could get so bad. He never cared enough to come to me. To share it. Maybe he meant to keep it from me. Maybe he thought he could deal on his own.

All I know is I fucking hate secrets.

And I have to find him. I've got two weeks to do it.

As I watch Lia play with the dogs under the

stars, I realize how much this house has come to mean to me. It's more than just my gramps's old place. A place where I could live and not have to worry about rent or where my next meal was coming from.

Since she moved in, this place has changed. It's not only the place Tim and I lived, not just the roof over our heads that we needed when we lost our parents. It's a place where I can see a real future for myself. A future that includes the MC, work that I care about, and a home. A home, I have to admit, that includes Lia.

Pretty soon, we won't have a fenced-in yard for the girl crew. We won't have each other. She'll move on to a new place, maybe with Morris and Alice, maybe on her own, or hell, even with Tiny.

I won't have anything.

Any stability I've created for myself over the last year is gone now. It's over. Tim has taken the only things that were ever really mine. Now, instead of everything I could have wanted, I'm going to have nothing.

Homeless.

No business.

No future.

No Lia.

Suddenly, there doesn't even seem to be a reason to fight. Not with Lia, not for her. I walk into the house and head straight for the kitchen cabinet. I fill a tumbler with whiskey and drop an ice cube into it. It's cheap stuff, so the ice will make it go down easier, but right now, all I want is to *not* feel. The sting of shitty booze won't hurt nearly as much as losing everything I have does.

I finish the glass, standing in the kitchen, leaning against the counter. Everywhere are signs of the life I've made in this house. In the fridge—the marinated chicken for a dinner I was supposed to make and all kinds of green shit that Lia makes into smoothies. The kitchen floor has six dog bowls, one for food, one for water—one each for each dog in Lia's girl crew. Those dogs have different water dishes outside and in the living room. I can't go into a room without seeing a disemboweled dog toy, loose stuffing, or a hard plastic bone. Lia's hairbrush or those endless ribbon hair-tie things she wears on her wrist and slips over doorknobs. The proof of a settled-in life is all around me. I can't believe shit's about to get upended.

I fill my glass again, this time not bothering with the ice. The first tumbler took the edge off, but this time, I want to go numb. Feel the burn of the alcohol and the long, vacant nothing of the buzz. Maybe that's what Tim's been chasing all this time. Something to numb the pain. The way I feel right now, I can't say I totally blame him.

I kick off my boots and drop onto the couch, finishing off the second whiskey in a few sips. I stumble to the kitchen for another refill, but this time, I grab the bottle.

"LEO…"

I can hear her voice, but I don't want to open my eyes.

"Leo, come on. It's midnight. You need to go to bed."

I crack my eyes open and see I'm surrounded by girls. The dogs are tucked in beside me on the couch and are sleeping. A light blanket has been tossed over my legs. I stretch and realize I'm still feeling the whiskey I chugged. I'm fine, a little sleepy, but not at all numb like I was hoping for. Opening my eyes and seeing Lia, I'm not numb at all.

"I'm all right," I mumble. "Gonna sleep down

here." I roll over onto my side and tug the afghan to my chin.

Lia has showered and changed into a sleep tank and shorts. She's sitting across from me in a chair, and she's watching me. Her damp hair trails down her shoulders and leaves little wet marks on the sleep tank. Her nipples are hard, and any other night, I'd be on her, tasting her clean, sweet skin. Drinking in the softness of her sexy body instead of losing myself to bad whiskey. But not tonight.

"'Night, Lia." I want her to go, to leave me. There's nothing more for her to say. Nothing for anyone to say.

"I'm here for you," she says. "You can talk to me."

I huff a sigh. "Nothing to say, babe. I'm gonna sleep."

I close my eyes and hope she goes upstairs and leaves me to my misery. But I feel her shoo the dogs from the couch. She climbs onto the couch and slides in beside me. She lifts up the blanket and snuggles in, spooning her back to my front.

This is new.

We've never done this before.

Snuggling?

I'm not talking about the after sex, before

someone needs to get up and get going kind of snuggling. The kind that fills the space after we blow each other's minds and come back to earth.

This is *new.*

"You okay?" I ask. The scent of her hair fills my nose, and I can almost taste her. Her skin, her nipples, her pussy. Everything about her hits me as she presses against me and settles in. My body lurches to attention, no longer trapped between sleeping and drunk. My dick throbs to life, and I snake an arm over her. "Hey, we'll be all right," I assure her.

"I know," she says, but her voice doesn't convince me. "I was thinking…"

Oh fuck. I blink my eyes open and take a breath. "Lia…"

"Hear me out," she says. "My mom sold her place. She's got that rich husband. Maybe they can help us. Josh won't have to take the house if they can give us the money to cover Tim's bail."

"No. It's not that simple. I mean, we're talking a hundred and fifty large for the bail. And I'd have to pay that money back to your mom or her husband or whoever. I don't think I'd be able to pay back that kind of money even if I had ten years to do it."

"Could you take a loan against the house?" she

asks. "Is there any way you can borrow the money?"

I nod, my nose digging deeper into her hair with every move. "Possibly," I tell her. "But it's unlikely I'd be able to get the money in ten days, even if I did get approved for a loan of some kind. There's not enough time. I wouldn't want to accept a loan from your family without knowing for sure I had a plan to get it paid back. And that's assuming they'd be willing to fork over that kind of cash to someone they've never even met."

Lia sighs and wriggles so her ass presses against the semi that's practically being strangled by my jeans.

"Maybe my dad…" She sounds like she's thinking out loud about this. "I mean, if he has the five thousand I need for my grooming certificate, maybe he's got…"

"No." That brings me up to sitting. That and the fact that my dick is not happy that it's trapped, with Lia's ass so close. "Listen to me," I tell her. "We are not, and I repeat, not involving your father or the MC in this in any way. You hear me? When I lose the house, I'm going to need the MC to give me a place to land for a while, but I will not go and bring my shit to the doorstep of the MC now. Not like this. The shit with my brother...the legal stuff."

I shake my head, even though the motion makes it throb. The club's trying to get clean. Lia knows this. Anything that brings us close to drugs or dirty money, the cops—that's a step in the wrong direction. And it's the best way to ensure my prospect days end with me handing back my patch.

And I'm not about to see that happen.

I can't even begin to think about that. Tim's drug problems and arrest...fuck that. The MC was already working to get themselves away from dirty money. We were cash poor and working to change all that. I can't drag my six-figure time bomb into the compound. This is the exact opposite of what the MC needs right now. This is my business, my house. The MC will be there after I have this fucked-up chapter in the rearview.

"I'll make sure you have a place with Alice and Morris, and if that doesn't work out..."

Lia is quiet.

"Lia, come on. Say something—"

I stop talking when she leans forward and kisses me. It's a sweet kiss, a kiss that says I'm sorry you're in this. I'm sorry you have to deal with this. It's a kiss that says she cares. For me.

I kiss her back, but something sweet won't satisfy me right now. She's nearly naked, and this may be one of the last nights we live together. As roommates. As this. As more.

"Lia…" Her name slips out after I release her mouth from mine.

She looks at me, all sadness gone from her face, and I know she wants me too. Maybe she's feeling the same sense of "What if this is over?" that I'm feeling. Maybe she's realizing she doesn't want this to end…just like I am.

I slide a hand beneath her hair and meet her eyes, but before the moment gets weird, I kiss her, opening her mouth so I can taste her. In seconds, the dogs are off the couch. Lia's sighing my name and tugging off her top between kisses. I pull my mouth away only long enough to unzip my pants and toss them on the floor.

When we're both naked, Lia settles back against the couch, and I grab her knees, lifting them onto my shoulders. I'm wound tight with need, a hunger to do something, anything, that will drive away the anger, the powerlessness I'm feeling. I take it all out on Lia's pussy. I plant my mouth over her clit and suck her in, swirling my tongue against the tight nub. I grip her thighs in my hands, and she spreads her legs wide open, giving me full access to feast on her.

She thrashes against the couch cushions, pressing her pussy against me harder, grinding against my lips and tongue. I lift my head to catch my breath and stroke my chin back and forth along her drenched seam. The light friction from my stubble has her wrapping her legs around my head and pulling my mouth even closer.

"Leo, fuck…" She's gasping. Her face is pink, her tits blooming with a flush that's blotchy and red, letting me know she's so hot, she's close to exploding.

I want more, though, harder, faster. I slip two fingers inside her and make long strokes against her walls, the bite of her nails into my shoulders letting me know my pace is perfect.

When I feel the gush of her release against my fingers and she cries out my name, I slow my speed and bite my way from her inner thighs to her lips. She's shuddering and writhing, riding out her climax, and I slip my fingers into my mouth so I can taste her juices. I kiss her, mingling the taste of her pussy with the taste of her berry-sweet mouth. Her legs are still trembling, but I take her thighs in my hands and bring her legs together.

Lia is as limber as a dancer. It's one of the things that makes her so much fun to fuck. I'll miss this when it's over. I know that much. We've got so many positions. We know each other's bodies so well now. When I lift her ankles in the air, she knows what I want. She crosses her legs at the ankle and holds them up high.

While she holds up her weight, I look at her sweet, wet pussy. With her legs scissored together above us, I know that sliding inside her, the pressure is going to be so tight, I won't be able to hold out for long. I kneel on the couch and brace my hands on her calves and angle my way inside. The first thrust is slow, me finding my way in and getting close enough that I can hold her legs up against me. Once I'm there, thrusting against the resistance of her weight...

It's fucking bliss. Pure, intense, immediate bliss from the moment my cock slides between her lips until I find my pace. I pummel my way home, my thighs pumping like pistons as I thrust myself into oblivion.

It's a desperate, emotional fuck. Lia's ankles are in my hands, and I'm blind with need. Eyes closed, I want to block out the look on her face. The arousal. The desire. She's exactly what I need, and it feels like this is what she wants too, because she tenses. I feel the pressure as she tightens around my dick.

"Fuck, Leo," she's panting, and we nearly fall out of sync as she takes over, shuddering as she rides out another climax.

I come fast. She's drenched and clenching my dick with her pussy with so much pressure, I couldn't hold out if I tried. The release tears through me, but I don't cry out her name, don't swear. I gasp for air and ride it, grateful for the loss of control. I let my body take over until it's done, collapsing against her. I'm sweating and shaking, but she's calm now, and she strokes my damp hair with a hand, carefully untangling her legs from my arms. I don't want to move. Don't want to get up, clean up. I close my eyes, and the booze make the room spin behind my lids.

I don't say a word. Neither does Lia. The house is silent except for the sounds of our breathing. The lights are on, but I don't want to get up. I shove a pillow over my face and roll onto my side, away from her. I said I was gonna sleep on the couch, and there's no reason not to, even now.

Lia backs up against me, her tits pressing against my back. She tugs the blanket over both of us, and the message to me is clear. Tonight, we break the habit of fucking and retreating to our own beds. Tonight, I fall asleep with her. For the first and probably last time.

When I wake up in the morning, Lia's gone. The house is quiet, and when I stumble upstairs to take a piss, the familiar steam and berry smell in the shower tells me she was up early and dressed. The dogs are gone too.

I check my phone and see I have a couple of angry texts from Tiny. I shoot one back.

Me: Personal shit came up. Be there in an hour.

Tiny doesn't respond right away, so I jump in the shower and get dressed. It's not that late yet, but it's odd that Lia didn't leave a note or send me a message. She did leave me a half-full pot of coffee in the kitchen, so I gratefully pour a mug to go and jump in my truck.

On the way to the MC, I start thinking. Thinking hard. I've got no answers for Tiny about the tenant situation. For a hot second yesterday, I thought Arrow could be a possible way out of the trouble with the building. Now I know I've got no leads on a tenant, and I'm about to lose my house.

Not to mention Lia. Last night was nice—fucking awesome, actually—but I hope scratching that itch doesn't make things weird between us.

I pull into the compound and park my truck, sunglasses blocking the glare from making the threat of a headache into a full-blown problem. I grab my phone, and before I head inside, I fire off a text to Lia.

Me: Thanks for the coffee this am. See you at work?

I pocket my phone and head into the compound. I head straight for Tiny's office.

"Prospect," he grunts. "Status on getting us a tenant?"

I shake my head and drop into the chair. "Working on it. Thought I had a decent lead yesterday, but…I'll get there."

Tiny nods and goes back to whatever he was looking at on his phone. He's got his typical half-gallon plastic cup of whatever sugary cocktail he starts off the day with on his desk, and he seems as bored with me as ever.

When I don't get up, don't leave, he leans back in his chair. "You need something?" he asks.

Now may not be the time, but time is a luxury I don't have.

"Any chance I could hole up in a room here at the compound? If I needed to?"

Tiny's beady eyes narrow on me. "What'd you need a room for? What's wrong with your house?"

I nod. "Nothing's wrong. House is fine." That's not entirely a lie. The house is fine. It won't be mine for much longer. "I'm thinking…" I wasn't thinking, not before I opened my big mouth. But I'm thinking fast now. "There may be a time when my roommate wants the house to herself, date night or something. It could be good if I had a place of my own."

"My daughter's dating someone?" Tiny looks relieved and pissed all at once.

I shake my head. "Come on, Tiny. I stay out of Lia's business. I'm just saying, what if. Shit changes, you know?"

He doesn't seem to like that answer. "Change isn't always good."

Fuck if that's not right.

I nod. "No worries, man. I got some shit to do."

I stand to leave, but Tiny stops me at the door. "Prospect."

I turn to face him.

Tiny's standing, leaning with his full weight on his desk. "Sometimes I gotta wear two hats," Tiny says. "And I'm not a hat man." He looks me dead in the eye. "When I'm wearing the club hat, I can tell you that, once you're in the club, the club becomes your family. You're in need, we're here for you." He sniffs hard and raises his chin at me. "As a dad, you fuck with my daughter…" He lifts a brow at me. He shrugs and brings his hands together, cracking his knuckles.

"You can spare me the show, Tiny. I get it." I leave, not giving a shit if I've pissed Tiny off.

Right now, the worst he can do to me is nothing compared to the shit that's already on my doorstep. My phone buzzes with a text alert as I'm on my way to the kitchen to grab more coffee before I head out. I'm not doing any more work at the compound today. I came in, checked in, and now my real job is to find a tenant for the space while trying to find a way to keep the wolves away from my house. If the shitters need cleaning, they can wait.

I fill my coffee cup and grab my phone. The text is from Lia.

Lia: Get to work as soon as you can. I have news.

7

LIA

"LIA?" Josh pulls open the door. "I was surprised to get your call."

He scratches his head, and I hate him a little more when he does it. His hands are like model hands. Muscular, trim nails. Sexy. The guy's so built, even his palms seem thick with muscle. As much as part of me would love to feel those hands on my body, I'm leading this conversation with my heart.

"Yeah, well, thanks for coming by." I've given the dogs some chew toys so they'll keep the distractions to a minimum. "I did some research on Florida bail laws."

Josh nods. "And?"

"I'd like to see the backup for your claim against Leo's house. I want to see the paperwork."

Josh sighs and crosses his arms over his chest. His muscles flex, and I look away, steeling my resolve. I'm not here to eye-fuck the man or even to be nice to him. I'm here to save Leo's house and my home.

"Lia, look, I know what you're trying to do here. And it's great, okay? But I can't involve you in this. You don't have any rights to the house. You're not an owner. And even though you live there, I can't violate my client's privacy rights by showing you the paperwork."

"You can't violate your client's rights, but you can take Leo's house? My home. What kind of shit is that?" I start to get heated right away with him because it is bullshit. Pure and simple. "Maybe you can give me some advice, then? Should I be packing this week? Am I gonna be homeless in two weeks? Will Leo?" I start pacing around my shop, hoping that Josh feels like shit. I know this isn't his fault, but I'm sure he hasn't been up front with Leo, and he deserves to suffer a little for it.

"No. God, no. You—" Josh looks lost, unsure what to say.

"I thought you were a professional bail agent," I

say. "You must explain this stuff to people every day. Explain it to me."

Josh shakes his head. "Lia, this is really stuff that Leo should be handling. I'm sorry. I wish there were another way."

"Isn't there?" I'm not letting him get off the hook that easily. "Because I may not have experience with this stuff, but I can research."

Josh watches me as I open my laptop.

"There is all kinds of information out there. YouTube videos, blogs, websites. In fact, the way pretty much everyone out there makes it sound, you're the one who gets screwed if Tim doesn't show up for that court date."

Josh sighs but doesn't disagree. "What's your point in all this? Yeah, I'll be screwed if Tim doesn't show. But Tim has the legal right to put the house up for collateral, which means it's a pain in the ass for me, but I don't come out of this at a loss."

"You might." I lift my chin at him. "Tim owes what, like $150,000?"

Josh nods. "And fees and penalties and stuff. It could come up to quite a bit more."

"Have you looked at the tax records for the house yet? Have you looked to see what the mortgage is?" I have not done any of those things, and honestly, for all I know, Josh could have done them. All I do know is there's a really good chance that all the stuff I researched is going to buy us time, even if it doesn't get us out of this fully.

"Lia." Josh shrugs. "None of that matters. What matters is that we find Tim so that no one has to deal with the consequences of Tim's actions except for Tim."

"In theory, that would be great." I open up a local real estate office's website. "Check these out." I point to thirty-two houses for sale in Leo's zip code.

Josh comes close and leans over to get a better look at the screen. His cologne overwhelms my senses, and I shake my head and hand him my laptop. I need to put some space between us. He's the enemy, even if he smells like a sexy campfire.

"Lia, what does this have to do with Tim? Can you help me out here?" Josh lowers his voice, and for a second, I see the good guy in there. It makes me wonder why a guy like this is in this line of work at all.

"Why do you do it?" I blurt out the question before I realize how it sounds. "Why do you do this?

Why does a guy like you work around people who are in trouble all day long? People running from you? People *not* wanting to see you come through that door?"

Josh's face hardens.

I've hit a nerve. There's something there, something buried deep that I doubt he'll share with me, and I really don't want him to. I don't want to have any compassion or sympathy for this guy. He doesn't have any for us.

Well, maybe he does. He and Leo, they knew each other when they were kids, but a job's a job, and he's doing his so that he comes out on top, so that he benefits. And if that means he takes away the only stability that Leo has left in his life…well, I can't have compassion for that guy. No matter what his reasons are for being in this line of work.

"We all have our reasons for doing what we do," he tells me. He stands a little bit closer to me, and that damn campfire smell fills my nose.

I resist the urge to close my eyes and drink it in because, again, he is the enemy. "Okay, so if you're not going to tell me why you do it, maybe you'll explain a little bit more about how. I told you I've done the research. Now explain to me what really happens. I know there's gotta be a way out. There's gotta be a Plan B for Leo. A way for you to not take the house even if we never find Tim."

Josh smiles at me. It's a seductive smile, sweet, appreciative. He meets my eyes and nods at me. "Why don't you tell me what you understand, and I'll explain the details," he says. "Anything you want to know, I'll lay it out for you straight as far as I'm legally able."

That's a start. I'll take it.

"I lived on the road for a while," I tell him, "But in the past when I've rented apartments or rooms, it's always been a really big pain in the ass when you have a shithead roommate. Getting somebody out under any circumstances is next to impossible."

Josh looks at me. "Okay... And?"

"So," I continue, "let's just say we never find Tim. Court date comes and goes, and you get to claim the rights to Leo's house."

Josh smiles. "It's not exactly claiming the rights...but yeah. I'm with you. Okay, worst-case scenario happens. Tim is in the wind, and now I have a right to the title to Leo's house."

"Exactly," I say to him. "So, if I can't get rid of a roommate who won't pay the rent, how do you really expect to get Leo and me and three dogs out of a house in under two weeks?"

"I'm not following…" Josh says.

"That's what I was researching," I explain. "As far as I understand the whole process of getting us out of the house, even if you legally have the right to do so, it's going to take time. There's no way that you're going to kick us out, claim the house, sell the house, get access to whatever money is there— assuming there're no loans or liens against the house already. But if you can get enough at a fair sale to cover what Tim owes…" I point to the laptop screen. "Of all these houses in a ten-mile radius from Leo's house, do you see any that are selling or are listed for sale for more than what Tim owes?"

I give him a look, hoping he realizes I've done my homework here. Not being able to sleep last night—before I showered and Leo and I got naughty—was time I put to good use.

"What if the house sells for less than the bail?" My question is direct, with a hint of a challenge in my voice. "What, then?"

Josh nods. "Fair point." The looks he's giving me sizzle with heat. But he's not angry that I'm up in his face, challenging him about what he does for a living. What he's doing to Leo. To me. "You're getting into the weeds on the details, Lia. That's the right thing to do." He leans against the counter and crosses his arms over his chest.

I try again to make out the wall of dark images he has inked on his skin.

"And you're right about the timing," he admits. "Realistically, the court will allow a grace period for me to find him and even for Tim to show up. And when that sort of second chance expires, then, yes, to really go through the process of taking possession of the house, putting it up for sale, resolving the outstanding bail… Yeah, it could take some time."

I tilt my head at him. I hope, especially after all this, he doesn't think I'm stupid. "Come on, Josh, not just *some time*. This kind of stuff doesn't happen in two weeks."

He nods once, a curt agreement. "You've done your homework, Lia."

"If it takes you even six months to get the money that you need to cover what Tim owes you," I press, "that sounds like plenty of time for Leo to find a way to get the money he needs to cover that bail. If he can do that somehow—I don't know the financial ins and outs—but I'm only saying, it sounds to me like you're the one in trouble, not us."

Josh curls his lips, and even a face that was probably meant to be a sneer looks seductive. I need to look away, just look away, think about Leo. My sweet roommate. My best friend. My secret lover, sure, but that's not what this is about. This is about the fact that he has nobody to stand up for him. Nobody to do the research and challenge the wrongs that have been done to him.

If my going toe-to-toe with this tattooed Adonis is going to help save Leo's house, or at least show him that someone cares enough to step up and step in, I can fight my hormones and my traitorous body and try.

"Everything about this deal has been above-board, Lia," Josh says. "I haven't done anything to manipulate Leo, to lie to him, to misrepresent the facts. I'm sorry that you guys are in this shitty situation. I'm sorry Tim up and refused to honor his obligations. But I'm in the clear here. In fact, Tim has fucked me too."

His words do nothing to make me feel sorry for him.

"Being in the clear and being on the hook for that kind of money seem like two separate things from where I sit," I say coldly. "Is Leo's name on that house? Couldn't we fight you taking it if we hired a lawyer? Because we will."

I immediately think of the money Tiny offered

116

to give me for school. It's not enough to cover Tim's bail, but it should be enough to help us get some answers from someone who knows our rights.

The fact is that I'd give up my plans, my education, to save Leo's house. Oddly, it doesn't surprise me. Even while standing beside this stupidly sexy bounty hunter, or whatever the hell he is, Leo has a piece of my heart. Now's not the time to overthink it. I hope the threat of hiring a lawyer cools Josh off.

"You have every right to hire a lawyer," Josh says. He leans close to me, but it's not creepy, not suggestive. I feel like he's trying to be kind. "I can't say I disagree with you. I wouldn't be very comfortable right now if I were in your shoes. Or Leo's shoes. And you're right, I'm the one on the hook for Tim's bail. The issue of collateral and actually claiming it—it's not easy, not simple, not fast. I know that, and you do too. So now, what do you want to do about this?" He studies my face. "Because I don't think you would have called me here if you didn't have some kind of plan."

This is where my plan gets a little bit uncomfortable.

"Lia?" he presses. "What are you thinking?"

I play a little coy, stalling for time. I'm not sure that I trust Josh not to use any information I give him against us. But I'm sure that the best and fastest way to make things right is to find Tim. I close the laptop and look away from Josh. I want my head clear as I explain what I have in mind.

"We went to Checkers last night. That was a total bust. Part of me thinks that if Tim or this woman, this Juliette, this wife person, whoever she is —if she is hanging around, having Leo be anywhere near would be a red flag. If they saw him or his truck, they'd run for the hills. If they haven't already. But they don't know me from Adam. I've never met them, and I wouldn't know them if I saw them."

"Right," Josh says.

"Why don't you take me to Checkers tonight?" I ask.

I know even as I ask him that spending any time alone with the enemy like this should make me feel like shit. I'm doing this for Leo, though. For the good of the house. For the good of the two of us, one roommate to another.

I shove thoughts of Leo away, of the night we spent on the couch. I'm doing this for him, for Leo. Even if the idea of spending time alone with Josh feels like I'm doing something wrong.

"Let me get this straight." Josh's eyes sparkle,

and his tone lightens. "Are you asking me out a date?"

I give him a playful wink and shrug, making sure I toss my hair a little bit so my cleavage is fully on display. I might toy with Josh, but right now, my focus has to be on the goal. Saving Leo's house.

"I'm focused on helping my friend," I clarify. "I just want to find Juliette or, even better, Tim."

Josh tilts his head and grins. "Whatever you say, Lia," he says. "I'm in."

There's a slight twist in my stomach as he agrees. I guess part of me hoped he might refuse. Say it was too dangerous or not my place or something. But Josh may be as desperate as I am, as Leo and I are. We may be able to buy some time, but unless Leo's got money hidden under a mattress, which I know he doesn't, I don't see what other choice we have. I can at least try. Even if that means it feels weird, almost wrong.

"Okay," I say. "It's a plan." I stress the word *plan*.

"Should I pick you up?" Josh asks. "Seven o'clock? Your place?"

"Make it eight," I say.

"Eight, it is," he says. "And then what? Straight

to Checkers? We doin' dinner first, dinner after, what are we talking?"

I shake my head. He's definitely trying to date me. I sigh and put a hand against his chest and flutter my eyes at him. "You are something else, Josh Arrow."

"Aronowicz," he says, pronouncing his last name for me. "But I love to hear Arrow coming from your sweet lips."

I run my tongue over my lower lip and meet his gorgeous gray-green eyes. "Eight o'clock," I tell him, giving his chest a tiny shove. "Now, go. I have work to do."

Josh chuckles. "See you tonight, sweetheart."

After Josh takes off, I check the time on my phone. I'm surprised Leo's not back yet. He hasn't texted me back yet either, which makes me nervous.

But since I haven't heard from him this morning, I start to worry. Maybe he's mad. Maybe he doesn't know what to do after last night. We crossed a line.

But now I have to wonder…

"Excuse me?" A woman's voice startles me from my thinking.

"Hi, can I help you?" I ask.

She's a teeny tiny thing, and she immediately

bends down to pet my dogs. "I'm wondering if you do boarding here?" she asks. "Like overnight or longer stays? Can you tell me a little bit about your place?"

A customer. *Finally.*

"Yeah, absolutely." I come around and greet her warmly. "How did you hear about us? I'm still fairly new in business, but I'm thrilled you stopped by." My dogs are wagging their tails and snuggling up to her for attention. "Sorry about them," I say. "Tell me about your dog—or dogs?"

We chat a few minutes about how she found us —just driving by—and she has a large breed dog, which is why she's looking for a place big enough to give her black Lab room to run when she travels for work.

"Many places keep the dogs in kennels the whole time," she says.

I offer to give her a tour of the place, especially the outdoor area. "The back is fully enclosed, and any pets that stay with me for exercise or playtime have plenty of outside breaks during the day." I turn around to lead her on the start of my tour.

"What about overnight?" she asks. "Do you have any techs who watch the animals overnight?

Or would they be locked up all alone here overnight?"

She looks like any dog mama would—not too happy about her baby being left alone overnight.

"I don't have overnight staff yet," I explain, "but I have security cameras, so I monitor the dogs both on camera and with audio. If any of the dogs are sick or in distress, we would make arrangements with you beforehand to make sure they are taken care of with a specialized care plan. We do charge extra for that, but we can be flexible."

I show the woman the backyard and take her all the way around the property to show her that the back is fully secure. None of the dogs could get off the property while they are playing or taking potty breaks. We walk back around Leo's shop, and I notice he's still not in. As we pass by Alice's office, Alice lifts a hand to wave, and I wave back.

I can't wait to tell her I may have a new customer.

A new client and a plan to save Leo's house.

It's going to be a great day.

8

LEO

I SLIP my phone into my pocket, and before I leave the compound, I head over to Dog's room. His door is open, and he's sitting on his bed, cup of coffee in hand.

I knock. "Hey, man. You got a minute?"

Dog looks up at me and pushes a pair of reading glasses off his face. I have to laugh…these bikers. The old-timers are eighty-percent badass and twenty-percent old man.

If I'm lucky, that'll be me someday.

"Whatcha reading there," I ask. "*Wall Street Journal? New York Times?*"

"Fuck you," Dog says, holding up his cell phone. "I'm reading a romance novel."

I shake my head, cracking up. I wouldn't be

surprised if he was. Dog's got one of the biggest, most loyal hearts I've seen. What I wouldn't do to have a dad or an uncle like this guy. It's part of the reason why prospecting means so much to me. These guys are good men. Family men—both inside the compound and out there in the world.

"What you got for me, Prospect?" Dog asks. "Tiny riding your ass again? Need me to put some ointment on your cheeks?"

I laugh. That's a new one. "No, man. This is an electric question."

"What kind of electric?" he asks.

Everybody knows that Dog is the one to go to for any electrical problems on our bikes, cars, boats. He was a long-haul trucker for years until he was in a pretty bad accident. He doesn't work in the business anymore, but he's probably forgotten more about electrical systems than I'll ever know.

I explain the situation with the Cadillac. "When I opened the hood, it was clear that some kind of homemade shit was going on in there. Teddy bears, duct tape."

"What kinda dumb-ass shit you talkin' about, kid?"

"I'm kidding," I say quickly, "but not by much."

"How's it running if it's that bad?"

"It's not. Customer had it towed in, but I honestly don't know that I even have the skills to get it running again. I'm supposed to give her an estimate next week. I told her I'd need a couple days to run some diagnostics, price out some parts. But what's going on in there is nuts. I'd love a second opinion."

"You want me to come down to the shop, take a look at it?" Dog asks.

"When you can," I say.

He nods at me, and I return the gesture before getting ready to head in to work. My mind races as I get in the truck and drive over to the shop.

Lia's got news, but unless she's found my brother, I'm not in the mood for it. She's a sweet girl. She tries hard. I know she cares, but I'm not in the mood for sunshine and positive thinking.

As I pull into the parking lot of the building, I have to fight a sudden rush of feelings. I can't believe everything I've ever worked for I'm going to lose. A year ago, I went through the same damn thing when this building got taken away because Tim was a year behind on the mortgage. Gramps left everything in Tim's name because he was the oldest, and he trusted my brother to take care of me.

I always trusted Tim. Until now.

I'm only glad my granddad never lived long enough to see my brother turn to drugs. Never lived long enough to see my own brother let the only things we had slip through our fingers. I never thought I'd see the day when Tim would not only let me down, but that he'd screw me.

I'm so worked up over the fact that all of this is going away, that I'm getting fucked over again by Tim, I don't have time to think about how I'm going to feel seeing Lia this morning.

But when she rushes up to me, bouncing on her toes before I even get out of the truck, it all comes back to me. "Leo." She's flushed and looks so happy to see me.

It's hard not to feel a little better, but I'm not in the mood for light today. I don't know how to handle everything I'm feeling. The business, the building. The house. Now her. This.

"Hey." I nod at her and lock the truck. I walk past her and head toward the shop. She hasn't unlocked it for me today, and that immediately sets me off. "Why is the shop closed? Have you been covering the phones?"

Her smile fades. "No—I... I—"

I hold up a hand and shake my head. I unlock

the door and yank it open, walking away from her fading sunshine.

"Leo?" She follows me into the shop. "Are you angry at me?"

I don't know what I am.

Yes, I'm angry.

I'm fucking furious.

There's too much going on, and none of it is shit I can solve quickly or easily. I'm about to be homeless and make Lia homeless too.

My business—or what there is of it—is about to be the only thing I have to my name, and she let the store sit idle while she did God only knows what. She's a flake, yes, but she's normally more responsible than this.

"I got to get to work." I avoid looking at her and start flipping on lights. I turn on my old-ass computer and run some music through the tiny speakers I have set up on the counter. "Let's talk tonight at home."

"Leo…" She comes close to me, puts a hand on my shoulder. "Did you get my text? I did some digging, and…"

I shrug away from her touch. "Not now, Lia."

If I'm not gonna give her a chance to explain, I sure as hell don't want her touching me. Not now. I have enough confusing shit swirling in my head. I don't need my body and all the goddamn emotions Lia brings up making this even harder.

The look on her face about fuckin' guts me.

"Lia," I say, but my heart's not in an apology. I have the weight of the world on my shoulders, and I can't share this.

Not with her.

It wouldn't be fair to either of us.

She turns and leaves the shop without another word, and somehow that makes me feel even worse.

THAT NIGHT, I whip up the chicken I had planned to make for us last night. Around seven, I head upstairs with two cold beers. A peace offering.

I knock on Lia's bedroom door.

She opens it and walks away, the invitation to come in implied.

I drop onto the foot of the bed and crack open the beer. "Peace offering," I say and hand it to her.

She takes it.

"We still doing this?" I ask.

"What?" She's never been the game-playing type. "Doing what? Losing our house and treating each other like shit for the last few weeks we have it?" She crosses her arms and glares at me. "You tell me, Leo. Is this how you want this to go down?"

"Fuck." I pop the tab on my beer and down it before I say anything more. "I'm not trying to treat you like shit, Lia."

"An apology would go a long way for giving me the cold shoulder this morning," she says.

"Are you gonna eat?" I ask. "Made dinner."

"Will you be serving apologies? Or should I swallow my chicken down with a helping of *fuck you very much*?"

"Jesus Christ, woman." I stand and try to pull her close, but she pulls away. "You want to hear me say I'm sorry? I am. I am sorry, Lia. Sorry that I wasn't excited to listen to you earlier. Sorry that I'm so obsessed with finding my brother that I can't do anything but stress out about this house. Keeping us both from becoming homeless."

My words don't sound even remotely apologetic or sorry. And Lia seems to close off more the more I say. I decide to shut the fuck up and leave it be. I can't fix this for her. I can't fix this for myself. We're literally living on borrowed time.

"So, you can't listen to the research I did? What if I found out something that can help?"

"It won't help, Lia." I surprise myself by blurting it out. I run a hand through my hair, trying not to punch a wall, slam a door.

It would be so, so easy to drag this place down to the ground. Make sure both Tim and Arrow get fucked the same way they are trying to fuck me.

"How do you know?" Her voice is quiet. "You won't listen."

"Maybe I can't." I take the now-empty beer can in my hand and toss it against the wall.

It clatters weakly and falls to the ground, but the noise freaks out the dogs, and they start barking and shaking. Pixie hides under the bed.

"Feel like a man now?" Lia taunts.

"You know what? Fuck this. Fuck all of it," I say.

"Fuck me too?" she demands, her hands on her hips. "Is that what you're saying?"

"Been there, sweetheart," I say. "Did and done."

She looks horrified, offended. "Right. Bang buddies for the win. This feels like a real winning situation right here."

"Congratulations on shacking up with a loser," I tell her. "But don't worry about it. You're about to be done with all of it. This house, the secrets. Me.

You're about to be free, Lia. Just the way you like it."

She looks like I've punched her in the gut. Her face is red, and her lips are working as if she's struggling over which words to let out. Not me. I'm not working that brain-to-mouth filter another minute.

If I'm going to lose everything, I might as well end it my way. I'm not going to beg Josh not to take my house. I'm not going to load my problems on to the MC. And I'm sure the fuck not going to drown my sorrows in a woman I can't have. Don't have.

I'm done playing Mr. Mom to a roommate and her pack of animals. I'm done pretending that Tim hasn't hurt me. That losing everything is a chance to start over. I'm done with secrets. With hiding. With everything.

"You wanna eat," I snap, "Food's on the table."

I storm out of her bedroom and down the stairs, load up a plate, and slam my ass into my chair. I open another beer and shovel the chicken into my mouth. It's probably delicious, but I don't taste anything. It's like sawdust in my mouth. I need to focus on every movement.

Bite. Chew. Swallow. Repeat.

Eating without her sucks, plain and simple. We eat dinner together almost every night, but tonight, staring at the empty chair across from me, Lia's bare toes missing from their usual perch on the empty chair between us, I want to shatter every plate in the house. But I keep my cool, eat my food, and listen.

I hear the water running upstairs, and I know Lia's in the shower. I avoid thinking about her naked, showering the anger and rage away.

We almost never fight. We don't have a system in place. No cue so I know when she's over it. When she's ready to talk again. I don't know how to let her know if I'm over it, because right now, I don't know if I ever will be.

I choke down the last of my dinner and make up a plate for Lia. I cover it with plastic wrap because I'm fucking depressed but I'm not a complete asshole. I leave her plate covered on the table and head to the couch. I kick off my boots and prop my feet on the coffee table.

I get a text from Dog and read it over. He's got some ideas about that electrical problem I'm having at the shop and wants to talk through it in the morning. Asks me to meet him at the compound a few minutes early so we can discuss it.

I think about messaging Tiny. I type up a whole thing, letting him know I'll probably be needing a room, but I stop myself and toss my phone across the room.

Fuck it.

Fuck it all.

I'll ask Tiny for help when I'm dead and gone. He knows I asked about a room at the compound, but I'm still a prospect.

There's no point.

He'll take care of Lia when this shit hits the fan. I won't be surprised if I am out of luck on the MC front anyway. They are looking to bring in cash, not a deadbeat who lost his home and is barely making the rent on his shop.

Maybe I can live in the shop for a while. I could probably get a shower installed. I don't need a full kitchen. I'll fucking find a way.

I'm doom-planning for my future when Lia comes down the stairs. She's still in her robe. The dogs follow her every move, their collars jingling in a way that's annoying as ever but familiar.

I half expect her to make some smartass remark and try to bring things back to center between us, but she walks right past me and into the kitchen. She shuffles around in there and walks past me with a green smoothie from the fridge in her hands. She takes it back upstairs without a word.

Fuck.

This is gonna get harder before it's over. I'm sure of that much.

ABOUT AN HOUR LATER, there's a knock on the door. I'm barely watching whatever it is I put on television. The endless cop dramas and true crime shit they play on cable have me exhausted. I've got enough true crime in my own front yard.

I get up and yank open the door to the one man I never expected to see darken my door again.

"What the fuck are you doing here?" I ask.

Arrow flexes his arms over his chest and nods at me. "Hey, man," he says.

"Maybe it was only in my head," I say, "but I could have sworn I told you to get the fuck out of my life. At least until you fuckin' ruin it." I go to slam the door in his face when a voice behind me stops me cold.

"Josh, be right there," Lia calls down the stairs so we both can hear her.

Josh looks apologetic as the reality hits me.

"Of fucking course," I say. "You here to fuck

around with Lia? It's not enough that you want my house, you want my girl too?"

"Hey, man." Arrow holds his hands up in a gesture of surrender. "I'm not here for your house, and I thought she was definitely not your girl."

I make a mock-bell noise with my mouth and clap sarcastically. "Give the man his prize." I try to slam the door, but a cloud of perfume comes over me and I turn.

Lia's behind me, and she's got a hand on my arm. "Josh, why don't you wait in your truck?" she says sweetly. "I'm going to let the dogs out back for a minute. I'll be right out."

Josh presses his lips at me, as if saying anything is going to earn him a punch in the gut—which it might. He turns and heads back to his truck to wait.

When he leaves, I slam the front door with every ounce of strength I have. It clatters on the frame, sending Lia jumping and the dogs cowering under the furniture.

"Are you fucking dating him? Is that what you were so excited to tell me all morning? Are you planning to save my house by fucking the guy who wants it? I should have guessed. It's poetic, isn't it?"

I know I'm spewing poison at Lia. But fuck, this is next-level betrayal.

Her face falls, but her outfit tells me everything. Booty shorts. Low-cut top with billowy sleeves, the one with the shoulder cut-outs. Curled hair, the high-heeled boots. She looks gorgeous, and she looks like this for him.

For my fucking nemesis.

"Now you want to talk to me about Josh?" she asks. Her voice is low, quiet.

"Nope. Ain't nothing to talk about. You do you. Do him, if you want. Maybe he's got a house he won't lose."

I don't care how my insult lands.

I don't give a fuck.

I'm angry, but more than anything, I'm fucking gutted that the first hint that this roommates with benefits situation isn't exactly what she wants it to be, she's literally off on the arm of another guy. It's her right. I have no claim on her.

This is actually for the best.

I storm up the stairs. "Have a great fucking time," I tell her. "And don't worry about me. Feel free to bring your new boy toy back here to fuck. I won't be here."

She doesn't say a word, but she lets her dogs out in the yard to do their business.

When I hear the kitchen door close, the girls

run up the stairs, and Lia shuts them in her bedroom. Her heels clack down the stairs, and I hear the front door close.

I'm not proud of the way I treated her.

I'm not proud of the fact that I want to smash Arrow's face into pieces with my bare hands. The thought of Lia with him, out with him…it brings me to a place I didn't think I could go.

I look out my bedroom window and see her climb into Josh's truck. She leans over from the passenger seat and gives him a kiss on the cheek before leaning back and fastening her seat belt.

He turns on the truck and backs out of my driveway. And then, they're gone.

I wasn't fucking kidding.

I won't be here when they get home.

I know exactly where I need to go.

9

LIA

JOSH IS DRIVING with one hand on the steering wheel. He looks over at me with a concerned smile. "That was worse than awkward. You all right?"

I shrug.

I'm not okay. I mean, how could I be? I'm doing this for Leo. Because of Leo. If his house and life weren't on the line here, would I really be all dolled up and going to a dive bar with another guy? Even if that guy looks like Josh does.

It's a fake date, I think, but it's only fake emotionally. We need to look, act, and smell the part. And fuck, does he. I close my eyes and rest my head against the headrest, savoring his scent.

He's unlike Leo in so many ways—alluring, tall,

heavily inked. He radiates swagger and confidence, where Leo is all earnest and sweet.

To be honest, I don't want to decide which I find sexier, because Josh has his hand on my arm, and the sparks that shoot along my nerve endings make it really hard to think.

"Lia?"

Josh must have been talking to me as I zoned out.

"Sorry." I twist my lips. "That was bad. Leo, back there. Are you okay?"

Josh chuckles. "Absolutely. You want to talk about a game plan for tonight?"

"You know what Juliette looks like? You'll obviously know Tim if we see him."

"Seeing Tim out is unlikely," Josh says. "But, yeah, I'll know Juliette."

"We hang out. We act like two kids out for the evening. We have a few drinks, and we keep our eyes and ears open."

I realize as I'm saying it that I don't have a clue how to play detective or whatever it is we're doing. Part of me thinks this was a stupid idea, but I don't know how stupid it really is if Josh is going along with it.

"Do you think there's a chance we'll find them?"

It's the obvious question, really.

Are Leo and I screwed?

Is this really going to happen?

"Lia," he says. His voice is rich, soothing. It calms me after the raw anger in Leo's. "If I've learned one thing in this business, it's that people will always—and I mean always—surprise you."

No shit.

"Sometimes in a good way?" I ask. "I don't think I could stay in a line of work where I was constantly dealing with the worst in people. The disappointment."

Josh nods. He flicks on his blinker and angles his truck into the parking lot.

"Sometimes in a good way, yeah. But more often than not, they surprise me. Quick story before we go in."

I settle back against the cushy seat. I love stories, and if this one has a happy ending, I'm here for it. I need something to shove away the pain of Leo's words today.

"Lay it on me," I say.

He turns a little in his seat to face me. He's cut the engine so all I can see are the contours of his gorgeous jaw as he talks, illuminated by the neon light of the Checkers sign.

"When I first got into this business, I had a client—an old man. He'd done a lot of crime in his time, okay? This guy was no innocent. But when he was arrested, he was caring for his daughter's kids because—of course—his kid was locked up."

"The mom?" I'm stunned.

He nods. "Yeah." He chuckles. "It's not funny, but for a while, I had those people on the family plan. I bailed out the mom, she spent about eighteen months out until sentencing, and later, I handled her old man's case."

Damn. That makes me think of Tim and how desperate times and a lack of opportunity could devastate an entire family. I wonder if Leo has ever been tempted, would ever go down the wrong path.

"She had three kids, meaning the old man was a grandpa. When he got pinched, it was for something petty—to be honest, I don't even remember what it was. It wasn't violent. I think he stole copper wiring off building sites or some shit. But because of his long rap sheet, he got himself some decent time when he finally got sentenced."

I watch Josh talk while I try to push the worries

about Leo and his future out of my mind. He wouldn't end up on the wrong side of the law.

Not my Leo.

Although, after tonight, I honestly don't know if I know Leo the way I thought I did.

"Turns out, this guy had been working hard to turn his life around while his daughter was locked up. He finished an associate degree and applied to a four-year university. He didn't have the cash to go, but he got accepted."

"Before he went to prison?" I ask.

He nods. "Acceptance letter in April, I think, and by June, he's in lockup."

I frown.

It's like Leo.

Just when things looked up with Morris buying his building, Tim put his house in jeopardy. I hardly have the stomach to hear the end of this story. I know it's not going to happen to Leo the way it happened to this guy, but it's hard to separate the two stories, the two men.

The downfalls.

"His oldest grandkid, this girl named Sara, she starts a letter-writing campaign. She's able to get her grandfather accepted into a special program.

He graduates with a bachelor's degree while he's in lockup. Straight A's."

"Then what? Is he still in prison? Was the degree his happy ending?"

Josh shakes his head. "It gets better, babe."

A shiver snakes up my spine when he calls me that.

"I had lunch with the man a couple weeks ago. He's getting a master's degree, and the two oldest grandkids finished their educations. One is a cosmetologist with a shop in Key West. The middle kid has a great job in HVAC, and the youngest is taking after his gramps and is going to college."

"What about their mom?" I ask.

He lifts a brow. I can barely see the gesture in the dark, but I can hear his disappointed sigh. "Their mom won't be getting out any time soon. Hers is a pretty tragic story. But her kids and her dad—they found their way. Her dad's like sixty-four now. He has a nice little condo, a job. You know the stats about offenders who earn degrees?"

I shake my head.

"Guess how many convicted felons who go on for graduate degrees end up reoffending and going back to prison?"

"Half?" I guess, optimistic that the number is big.

Josh leans forward so I can see his smile in the small beam of the streetlight overhead. "Almost none," he tells me. "There are some, but the statistical likelihood that a felon who earns an advanced degree will reoffend is almost zero."

"Seriously?" I'm stunned by that. I've never so much as shoplifted a lip gloss. I can't imagine a life where you're driven to commit crimes is easy to leave.

Josh nods and unlocks the car. "Anything is possible," he says. "Sometimes people let you down hard—" he gives me a meaningful look "—but a lot of the time, people will do the right thing."

I nod and grab my purse.

Checkers looks full tonight. I'm wearing my sexiest lingerie under this clubbing outfit, and I can't say I feel good about it. I feel conflicted about the fact that I would, on any level, dress like there was a chance Josh would see me in sweet under-things—or maybe in less—at all. Especially when, just this morning, I woke up in Leo's arms.

But that's ancient history. No—a mistake.

Leo's made it clear that if he remembers we slept together, like all night, it doesn't mean anything to him. We're roommates, for only a short while longer. And that's it.

That's how it has to be, so there's no harm in me feeling sexy around Josh. Even for Josh.

He comes around and opens the door for me, and I take his hand as he helps me out. His palm is dry and smooth—not rough at all. And so, so strong. I fantasize again how those hugs, and how muscular palms would feel spreading my thighs wide. But I shove those thoughts aside and focus on the task at hand.

Tonight, I may want Josh, but I'm here with another target in my sights.

One that's a lot less dangerous than Josh Arrow.

THE CLUB IS EXACTLY the way I remember. It's dark, and the conversations are muted, low.

"Is your girlfriend going to try to knife me in the bathroom?" I ask, thinking back to the chick who'd been all over Josh's lap the other night.

Josh squeezes my hand and motions for me to go in front of him toward the bar. "She's not exactly a girlfriend. She's not even a friend."

"A client?" I ask. "You never stop networking,

do you?" I nudge him in the ribs to let him know I'm teasing, and he rewards the gesture with a hand against the small of my back.

The touch of his hand literally sears me through the thin cotton of my slouchy top. My knees weaken, and I have to practically cross my legs to stop the flood of arousal. We have chemistry, and it's electric. But my heart doesn't want to follow where my body is demanding to go.

My nipples start to ache, that sharp, needy throb that begs for a mouth or a pair of strong hands to squeeze my tender skin. I don't know if Josh feels it too, because he pulls his hand slightly away and nods at me.

"Beer?" he asks, sliding past some rough-looking bearded dudes to get to the bartender.

I nod. He could have offered me motor oil at that point, and I would have thankfully sipped it, grateful to have something to focus on instead of him.

He orders two beers, and we stand at a small two-top table. There are no chairs in the place, so we stand facing each other. Josh scans the crowd while I pretend to entertain him with small talk.

Minutes feel like hours, and I don't think we're accomplishing anything. The woman in the black jeans who was all over Josh last night walks past and gives a casual "Hey" to him and a not-at-all-discreet glare to me.

I start giggling, and Josh drains the last of his beer, and takes mine and finishes it off.

"Come on," he says. "Let's talk."

He takes my hand and pulls me into the middle of the bar. The music is blaring something that we really can't dance to, but Josh is laying it on thick. He calls me baby and pulls me close, wrapping his arms around me and resting his hands right above my ass.

"This okay?" he asks in a whisper. "We're looking a little too interested in the crowd."

"This is your excuse for wanting me to look interested in you?" I give him a sultry smile, but I lean into his hold. "All part of the pretense?" I ask.

"All part of the pretense," he echoes. "Purely for show. There's no way any of this is real."

As he says that, he leans down and plants a featherlight kiss on my forehead. Not my lips. Not my neck. He kisses my forehead like I'm something precious to him. Something he treasures. And as sweet as it is, it feels wrong.

I know what it's like to feel treasured. Leo shows

me in a thousand things he does every week—every day, even.

At least, he did. He used to. The way he treated me today and into tonight, it's hard to say. Maybe hard times bring out the worst in him—or they bring out what's most genuine in him. I've never known Leo to go through any kind of real problems before this. And if this is the guy he becomes when the going gets tough…I could do worse than let Josh give me a peck on the head. A lot worse.

The music changes and the song slows down, so we're not as awkward out there swaying in each other's arms. Josh's cologne fills my nose, and my body reacts. I want him. I have to admit it. And is that such a bad thing?

I'm not saying I love Leo. I haven't said that to anyone in a really long time. But wanting a man and loving one are two separate things. After what I've seen from Leo, I'm lucky I know the difference. Or I'd be nursing a massive heartbreak right now, and who knows how different it would be to sway in Josh's arms.

I want to make small talk to break the tension between us, but anything I say feels like the wrong door to open. Leo and why we're here. Josh and his work. Which leads right back to Tim and to Leo.

Will I ever be able to talk to this guy without it feeling all wrong?

Without feeling like I'm doing something wrong?

"So, your dad's in a motorcycle club?" Josh cuts the tension for me, basically pouring a bucket of ice over my libido by bringing up my dad.

"Uh, yeah," I say. "But to be honest, I don't know much about that part of his life. I only really started to get to know him about a year ago."

Josh nods. "Not surprising. If you were mine, I'd keep you far away from the dangerous parts of my life too."

What was that? Do my ears deceive me? Or is Josh making a subtle dig against Leo? The situation we're in is not his fault. There would be no dangerous parts of Leo's life if he didn't have a deadbeat brother.

The MC surely isn't, but I know most have that reputation. Whatever Josh thinks about Leo, or the MC, he sounds like he's trying to drive a wedge between Leo and me. And part of me wants to go with it. Let Josh carry me past the memory of my roommate's sultry massages, deep kisses, and climax-worthy skills in bed.

"From what I've seen so far, that would mean I

couldn't be yours." I lay it on thick. "Your whole life seems dangerous."

Josh laughs, and the spark ignites between us again. "It only seems that way," he says. "I try to keep the criminals in prison, if they belong there."

I nod, but then, in spite of myself, I huff a long, sad sigh.

"Hey." Josh removes a hand from my back and tilts my chin. "It's all going to work out," he says. "I know it seems impossible now, but remember the grandpa felon who went to grad school. The road might be full of potholes, but you'll make it. Wherever it is you want to go." He meets my eyes, and something smolders there. "Deciding what you want might be the hardest part of all."

If I tip my head any farther back, he'll kiss me. I know he will. I can feel the heat from him every time our thighs bump. I let my hands fall from behind his neck, and I lean against his chest, burying my nose against him. If I don't bury my face, I may kiss him myself. And that's a complication I don't want, no matter how good and right his body feels.

"Lia," he whispers.

We sway together until the song ends, and Josh, thankfully, pulls back.

"You want another beer? I need something to cool me off. Like an entire swimming pool."

I nod, thankful that he's fighting whatever this is as much as I am. At least for now. "Same, but a beer will have to do."

Whatever this is—or isn't—with Josh, I can simplify it if I remember two things. One, he's not Leo.

And two, Leo means something to me. No matter how shitty he was to me today, he's never not listened to me before. He's never not taken my opinion seriously or treated me with anything less than respect and friendship.

He's going through shit, and I'd be a hell of an asshole roommate if, after our first big fight, I jumped in bed with Leo's enemy. In a few weeks, when things settle down, my emotions will be a lot clearer. And so will all of our intentions. Even mine. I can keep my body in check until then.

"I'm going to run to the ladies' room. Be right back." I give Josh's hand a squeeze before I release it and head to the back of the bar.

The tiny bar bathroom is dark but surprisingly clean. I can barely see to check my lipstick in the mirror, but I do it anyway. I smooth my hair, pop a breath mint, and head into the stall to take care of my business. While I'm in there, the door opens and I see one set of feet stop at the mirror. Another set goes into the stall next to me.

When I come out to wash my hands, the hard-looking chick Josh had on his lap last night is standing in front of the mirror.

She meets my eyes and nods.

I nod back.

I wash my hands and am reaching for a paper towel when she points at me.

"You Josh's girl?"

I shrug. This isn't the first time I've been cornered by some ho in a bar bathroom, thinking she's going to bully me out of being interested in a man. "He's only a friend," I say. "If you have something to say about it, you should take it up with him. He's right outside."

I go to leave, but she stops me with a hand. "This isn't about Josh," she says.

I flick a quick glance at the shoes in the stall behind me. My stomach sinks as I realize the door isn't even closed all the way. Whoever is in there isn't there for the toilet.

I clutch my purse over my chest and turn to leave the bathroom. I reach for the handle to yank open the door, but before I can leave, the stall door flies open and the man with the scarred hand I was talking to last night at the bar comes out.

He has a white cloth in his hand, and the only thing I hear before the room goes completely dark is his voice in my ear.

"Don't scream."

10

LEO

As soon as Morris answers my text, I pull on my leather vest, jump on my bike, and head to his new place.

The night air is clear, and I take the long way to his house. The way I feel tonight…I could jump on my bike and ride until all of this shit is far behind me.

Ride off into the night.

Hit the road and never come back.

When I finally pull up into Morris's driveway, I check the time on my phone. It's almost ten. Zoey will probably be sound asleep. I slip my phone into the pocket of my vest and knock once on the door.

Morris opens up, shirtless and barefoot. He's got

154

a pair of reading glasses on, and he looks like I've caught him by surprise.

"Shit, man, am I too late? I took the long way here to clear my head a bit…"

"Fuck no." Morris shoves the reading glasses on top of his head and waves me in. "I told you to get here when you get here."

I follow him to the living room and take a seat. He drops the glasses on the coffee table and gives me a look. "You tell anyone about these, Prospect…"

I chuckle. "Now I know what to get you for Christmas. One of those beaded chains so you can keep your cheaters around your neck. It's a good look."

Morris shakes his head. "Go fuck yourself. You'll get old too. I was reading a bedtime story to Zoey."

"Shirtless?" I ask.

He shakes his head. "Don't ask. Alice got this lavender hand lotion for Zoey. It's supposed to soothe her before bedtime like aromatherapy or some shit. She's going through a bit of a phase right now. I was handing Zoey the bottle so she could put some of that sleepytime lotion on while I read her the story, but the cap wasn't all the way on. I squeezed the tube and—" He makes a fart sound with his mouth. "Lavender lotion all over my shirt."

He stands up and heads for the kitchen. "I got a tee in the laundry room. Lemme grab it. You want a beer while I'm back here?"

"Nah, thanks, man." I settle back against their unbelievably comfy sectional.

I can't believe this is Morris's life now. Framed pictures of him, Alice, and Zoey line the walls. On the big-screen television, some animated show is frozen on pause halfway through. There are pink glittery things everywhere—jelly shoes, hair thingies. Living with Zoey and Alice looks a lot like living with Lia, except the glittery things in my house belong to a woman, not a kid.

I'm happy for Morris. This place feels like home.

When Morris comes back from the kitchen, he's wearing a wrinkled gray T-shirt and is holding two beers.

"Gotcha one anyway," he says, setting it on the table in front of me. "You don't want it, I'll polish it off."

I nod at him and decide to take it. I lift the bottle and tap the neck against his. "Thanks."

Before I get to the reason for my late-night interruption, a blur zips down the staircase.

"Uncle Leo?"

Zoey launches herself from a couple feet away and leaps into my lap.

I cough at the impact. "Kiddo. You're getting almost too old for uncle tackles. Are you sure you're not playing football at that new school of yours?"

Zoey giggles and hugs me hard. She's seven now and a serious doll. She's bright and sweet and has really come out of her shell since her mom left that dickhead stepdad and got herself hitched to Morris.

"Zoey," Morris says, shaking his head. "This is our new thing. We call it the distraction show." He checks an imaginary watch. "And the show is supposed to be long over by now…"

Zoey grins like she's been caught, but she plows right ahead with questions. "So, Uncle Leo, I have a question."

"No, you don't," Morris says. "Not after your bedtime, you don't. Ask Leo another time."

"Come on, Dad."

My heart nearly stops in my chest when she calls him that.

"*Dad*," I echo, laying it on for Zoey's sake. "Come on, just one question."

Morris sighs and looks up at the ceiling. "You don't know what you're getting yourself into, man. Zoey doesn't play softball. She goes for the tough ones."

I think whatever a seven-year-old can come up with, I can handle.

"Give it to me," I say. "Ask away."

Zoey's in a cute little two-piece pajama set that has ballerinas on it. She traces the swirling ribbons and patterns with her fingers while she seems to rack her brain for the best thing to ask her uncle Leo.

"So, when babies are in their mommies' tummies, how do they eat food?"

Oh God. I look at Morris in a panic.

He lifts a brow at me and takes a long sip of his beer. "Told ya. Good luck with that one."

"Well," I say, trying to think of how to answer that. "The baby eats food that the mom eats." I try to go basic.

"Yes, I know that. But how?" Zoey looks like she's worrying over the question. "Like, if the mama swallows the food and it goes into her tummy, does the food spill over the baby, and the baby just, like, opens its mouth and eats it? Like, the baby doesn't have any teeth. How can it eat, like, a cheeseburger? And doesn't it…"

"Okay, Zoey." Alice's voice carries through the living room. She's headed downstairs with a teddy bear in her hand. "I thought you were going to give Uncle Leo a kiss goodnight, not ask for an anatomy lesson."

"What's an anatomy lesson?" Zoey asks.

Alice quirks an eyebrow and points to the bear. "Mr. Pig here is ready for bed. That means you need to scoot your bottom back up these steps too."

I look at Zoey. "Wait. Your teddy bear is named Mr. Pig?"

Zoey starts laughing hysterically. "Yes. Leo, I thought you knew that. The bear is named Mr. Pig, and the pig is named Mr. Bear."

"She wants to know the ins and outs of human reproduction, but then takes a very literal approach to naming her plushies," Morris adds.

"They're best friends forever, and they decided to swap names because they love each other so much. Is that what you and Lia did? Lia, Leo?" Zoey looks as if she's unearthed one of the secrets of the cosmos.

Her little mind looks blown.

My little mind is blown too. Does everyone

CHELLE BLISS

think Lia and I are best friends and "love each other so much"?

Alice comes in with the save. "Unless you want Mr. Pig and Mr. Bear in a time-out, I'd suggest you give out some goodnight hugs and kisses. For real this time." She punctuates the statement with a mom look that lets all of us know she's not kidding.

Zoey throws herself against me, and I hug the little girl and plant a kiss against her hair.

"Night, Zo," I say. "We'll talk about how babies eat cheeseburgers another time."

Zoey starts cackling so hard she collapses against the couch.

"Okay, somebody's got a case of the sillies, and it's kicking in bad." Morris stands up and picks up the little girl in a firefighter move. "Train to Zoey's bedroom departs now."

He stomps away loudly, carrying Zoey up the stairs. Alice blows me a kiss and follows Morris back upstairs.

I'm alone for a few minutes sipping my beer. I can hear their voices carrying through the house. Morris's voice, low and serious, as he says whatever he's saying about Mr. Pig and Mr. Bear.

Alice's softer voice is light. She's laughing at Zoey's slaphappy giggles.

The entire scene is so normal.

So happy.

This is a real family.

Morris stomps down the stairs as my phone rings. An unknown number comes up on the caller ID, so I send it to voice mail and silence the ringer.

"So," Morris says, sitting back on the couch. "How are you, kid?"

I nod at him. "I'm all right."

"Tiny treating you okay?"

I shrug. "Does Tiny ever treat me okay?"

Morris nods. "He's tougher on you than he needs to be. But you live with his daughter. He's got to make sure he's doing right by his club and his kid."

"Doing right by his kid? Why? Does everybody think Lia and I are fucking?" I dart a glance at the stairs, hoping Zoey didn't hear me say that.

Morris doesn't respond, only takes a sip of his beer and gives me a look.

I sag back against the couch. "Come on. We're roommates."

Morris nods. "That you are." He's doing everything in his power to say as little as possible.

"This thing with Tim," I say, pivoting. I haven't told Morris about the latest shit Tim pulled.

It's embarrassing, degrading even. But it'll sure draw the conversation away from Lia and me.

"Something new? Something else? You heard from that piece of shit?" Morris asks. "If he's coming sniffing around the building…"

I shake my head. "It's not that. It's the house this time."

Morris's expression darkens. "What about the house?"

I explain a little about what's going on. Arrow coming to see me. The house being put up as collateral against Tim's bail.

"Goddamn." Morris looks stunned. "We've got options." He immediately leans forward and starts making plans. "Tomorrow, we go to Fingers, the club attorney. You got the papers? Let's start by making sure this whole thing is legit. You know this Josh from way back? You trust him?"

I shrug. "He's a high school buddy of Tim's. I don't have any reason not to believe what he told me."

Morris sniffs hard and grabs his phone. "Fuck, kid, if it weren't after ten, I'd call him now."

"No, Morris, that's not why I'm here."

He looks a little guarded. "What? You want money?"

"No, no, fuck no." I shake my head and hold up my hands. "I wouldn't take your money even if you offered it. I really wanted to…"

I don't know what I wanted.

Lia's out on a date with Josh.

My family is gone—all gone.

"You did the right thing coming here." Morris stands up and starts pacing. "I wish you'd come to me, what—when did this happen?"

I chuckle. "It's been like a day. It's not like I've been hiding this."

"No, son," he says, the word sounding so easy and right coming from him. Not paternal and patronizing, but kind. "But you've been carrying this. Alone. And that's not right."

He clenches his fists and flexes his massive biceps. Where Tiny is huge and round, Morris is muscle. "I wish I got my hands on this brother of yours a year ago."

"Me too," I say. "Me too."

"Know how to find him?" Morris presses. "It's the easiest way. You find this fuckup. Blood or not, he's fucking you solidly up the ass. You find him, and you turn his junkie dick in too."

"Wish I could," I said. "Wouldn't hesitate to

send his ass away, especially if it means keeping the house."

I think about telling Morris my plan. "I've been thinking about just…going."

"Going where? Where the fuck you want to go?" Morris looks confused.

I shrug. "Anywhere the road takes me. Just ride a while?"

Morris's scoff nearly sears the hair on my ears. "You serious? You're going to hit the road?" He paces the living room harder, and I'm wondering how he's not getting rug burns in his bare feet. "That's fucking bullshit, man, and you know it. You have a business, you've got a house. You've got a family here, Leo. What would Zoey think if her uncle Leo up and left? Ran off?"

"Well, I wouldn't have to answer any more questions about gestation."

Morris nods. "You and I both want that, but not that way. Listen." He comes around the couch and sits across from me, crossing his legs and dropping his heels onto the coffee table. "I know things have been dicey for you this last year. I get that. I was your age once, and I didn't think too much farther than the handlebars on my bike. I wanted to fuck three different women in one weekend, I did it. Bar fights, make money, lose money... You name it, I did it. And that shit was right for me. But look at all the years I spent drinking too much. Throwing away precious years I could have had someone like Alice, someone like Zoey in my life."

His eyes never leave mine as he continues. "I'm not telling you don't be young. I'm not saying don't get on your bike and ride off, in some kinda 'don't be like me' lecture. I'm saying don't do it because Tim's got you backed into a corner. Don't do it as a reaction to some other asshole's bad decisions. You wanna get on your bike and ride, I'll take the first leg of the trip right there with you, brother. But don't you even think about running away. A man stays. Faces his problems and kicks them in the nuts. And then, and only then, when you've given everything you have to the people you love and to the things that matter to you—if you want to walk away, at least it will be on your terms. Leaving nothing on the table."

I can't look at him anymore. I listen, letting his truth soak in. I haven't had a talk like this with anyone in so, so long. Only Lia. But somehow, coming from Morris, this lands different.

"Let's talk about Lia," Morris says. "Fuck the house. Let's assume you don't give a shit about the house and you're fine with this fuck-all taking it over. Fine. Lia's a good woman, Leo, and whatever you two think you've got going on over there, she loves you. Every single one of us knows that. Why do you think Tiny's so hard on you?"

"Why?" I ask. My stomach is tense now as we move the conversation to Lia. I haven't been honest with anyone about her, about what we've got there. About how I feel. Fuck, I probably haven't even been honest with myself.

"A man knows when his daughter's in love with a no-good biker." Morris cracks a smile. "Think about that, Leo. Think about her before you leave. She's a good woman, a beautiful woman. She'll be all right. She'll find someone else. But do you really want to walk away from her? She's under *your* roof. She's *yours* to care for right now, roommate or what-not, whatever you kids call these mixed living situations."

"Mixed living?" I practically choke on my laughter. Morris really is showing his age.

"Whatever." He waves a hand in the air. "Guys and girls not married, not fucking roommates. Call it what you want. But do you really want to take a chance on losing her when all you have to do to keep her is not give up?"

When I think about Lia, sitting here in Morris's house, my palms sweat, and my chest feels tight. We could have this, couldn't we? We could. If she weren't out with Josh tonight.

"I may have already lost her," I admit.

"In two days?" Morris says. "I haven't seen her in a day or so, but I don't think there's anything that could come between the two of you in twenty-four hours."

Morris hasn't met Josh "Arrow" Aronowicz.

"If you do get on your bike and go, be sure you haven't held anything back. That's all I'm saying."

"It's a hell of a lot of money, Morris," I remind him. "My house…"

"Fuck the house. They take that too, you move in here or get a room at the compound. A man doesn't walk out on his family. Ever."

I feel like this is a message about the club as much as it is about Morris, Alice, Zoey, and Lia. But it doesn't upset me or piss me off. It makes me realize that maybe I have more here than the left-overs of my brother's bad decisions.

"It's getting late. You've got a wife and kid." I drain my beer and stand up. I'm not mad. I'm not pissed off by anything Morris is saying.

I need time.

Time to think.

"If I know Zoey, she's asking for one last question. I'd better get up there and play bad cop."

"Right." I'm sure Morris is the Mr. Pig in the situation. A tough bear on the outside, but a plushie inside.

I take my empty beer bottle to the kitchen and toss it into the recycling bin. The fact that I know where it is and that Morris expects me to do that reminds me that I really am family here.

This may not be my house, but here, I'm at home.

I head back to the front door where Morris is waiting. "Prospect." He stops me with a hand on my shoulder. "You go if you've got to go. A man has to make his own way, and sometimes starting over is the only way. But going and running ain't the same. Choose the kind of man you're gonna be."

I nod and thank him for the beer. I head out to my bike and watch while the lights inside Morris's house turn off one by one. Finally, I see a bedroom light go on upstairs, and I back out of the drive.

I don't want to head straight home, so I ride through the deserted streets, thinking about my future. What I want. My house means something to me, but Morris is right. It's only a house. The place

I've laid my head since I was a kid, lost and without a family.

Maybe losing that place will be a blessing in disguise.

A new start.

A fresh start.

The harder thing to admit is how I feel about Lia. She's never been just convenient. She's never been just a roommate. But goddamn, sleeping with someone you live with is complicated. It's not like we've ever even dated. We were friends and room-mates first. How do you change something that's not broken?

Maybe how isn't as important as why.

Changing what we have so we can have more…

Morris is right.

What I have is worth fighting for.

What I want is not the house.

Not the business.

I'll work my way back somehow, if I have to scrub Tiny's toilets for five years to earn his trust.

And the house? I'll live some place. I'll work harder, fix cars faster, take on side projects. What I've got is worth keeping, and what I lose was never really mine anyway.

The only thing that stands in the way of my future is Arrow.

I may not be able to fight him on the house shit, but I sure as fuck can fight him for Lia's heart.

As I round the corner and head up my street, I realize I won't have to wait too long to fight Josh for Lia's affections.

His fucking truck is parked in my driveway.

11

LIA

WHEN I OPEN MY EYES, everything is dark. I try to open my mouth, but there's something keeping it closed.

The last thing I remember is using the bathroom. I was going to splash some cold water on my neck, cool down the heat from dancing with the enemy, and then…

I hear a woman's voice echoing someplace beside me. She sounds far away and yet close at the same time. Then I remember.

The bathroom.

The woman in the shredded jeans who was grinding on Josh's lap the other night.

The second set of shoes in the stall next to me.

Then everything went black.

My eyes are open, but it's so dark. I struggle to make sense of the shapes that spin before my eyes. If I look up, I can see streetlights passing. Windows. I can feel that we're moving.

I'm woozy and dizzy. Opening my eyes makes the sensation rolling around in my belly kick up.

I keep my eyes closed while I try to calm the immediate panic that forces my heart rate into high gear.

"She's up," the voice says, loudly this time.

Goddamn it. It's the woman from Checkers. That skank who had herself slathered all over Josh's lap.

A male voice from the front seat jump-starts my frantic pulse again. "Keep her quiet."

That voice is familiar, but I'm not sure who it is.

I try to talk, but all that comes out are mumbled sounds, trapped behind duct tape or whatever it is they've put over my mouth.

"Stay quiet," the woman barks. "Make a sound, and believe me, he'll stop the truck before we get where we're going. And I don't think you want that."

They're taking me somewhere.

The reality starts to hit me, and I can't help it, I'm struggling against the restraints to try to sit. My

172

feet aren't bound, but I'm not going to be able to do much more than sit up.

"Listen up, bitch." The asshole in the front looks back at me in the rearview mirror. I can see him trying to meet my eyes. "Stay cool. We don't want to hurt you. Keep quiet and let us do our thing. We'll let you go once we have what's ours."

Have what's theirs? I don't know who the hell these people are, let alone what they want. Or what they think I have that's theirs, but I can't exactly have a conversation about it…not like this.

I lie back against the seat cushions, my face pressed into the seat. If I could just sit up, I could at least see where they are taking me, but I'm on my side with my hands in front of me, and the night sky and a few streetlights are all I can make out. I try to watch for any street signs or other landmarks through the windows. The few signs I can see go by too fast for me to read.

And within a few minutes, the sky gets darker, the lights fewer and farther between. There are no more signs. Nothing to tell me where I am or where we're going.

Where they're taking me…

I rack my brain to think about what happened

at the bar. Who these people could be and what they could want?

Their faces aren't covered. I may not be a true crime junkie, but I know enough to know they probably have no plans of letting me leave. Ever.

My purse is still slung over my chest, which means my wallet and phone should be close by. I can't tell if they've gone through the bag, but it'll be good if my phone is still there. I try to shift my elbows a bit and get my fingers within reach of the zipper, but the woman beside me barks a laugh.

"Don't bother," she says. She holds up a glittery, charm-laden phone in its custom carrying case. She has my wallet too and looks damn happy about it.

"What do you want?" I grit against the tape over my mouth, but it comes out as an incoherent jumble.

"Shut. Up," the man up front says. He reaches up to adjust the mirror, and I catch a glimpse of the scars on his hand.

My eyes widen. I do know who he is.

Shit. Fuck. Goddamn.

It's the man I was chatting up at the bar last night.

How the hell these two know each other and what they want with me is a mystery, but it's one I

174

don't have much time to think about as the truck veers sharply around a curve. I have no way to stop myself, and I roll off the bench seat, falling roughly into the footwell of the back seat.

"Damn it, B," the woman hisses. I'm not sure if the woman beside me almost says the guy's name or if B is something they've agreed she'll call him. If she was about to say his name, she stops herself at that single letter.

"Problem?" he asks.

She shakes her head. "Dumb bitch fell off the seat."

He barks an order, loud, obviously directed at me. "Stay where you are. Don't try to move."

I do as he says, even though my head is throbbing from being banged around. The footwell is wide open, but it's dirty, leaves and muck back here on the plastic mats.

I try to support my head and neck without causing myself too much pain until the truck stops sharply and the guy in the front gets out. He slams the door, and I listen, praying they won't pull me out of the truck to hurt me. They want something. I tell myself, until they get it, they have every reason to keep me alive. Otherwise, they could have killed me in the bathroom and left me at the bar.

"Get out," the guy huffs, but I don't move.

He grabs my arms and yanks me out of the footwell of the truck.

I yelp in pain, but again, sound doesn't really come out. I try not to use my mouth, because when I do talk or move, it makes it harder to breathe through my nose.

I need to stay calm.

Breathe through my nose.

Stay aware of my surroundings.

I spent a lot of time alone on the road before I settled in with Leo. I was never in any kind of trouble like this, but I've been in some tight spots before.

All that matters is taking it moment by moment.

The thought of Leo brings a sting of tears to my eyes. He and Josh have got to know something's happened by now. There's no way someone could take me out of the bar and Josh not realize something was very, very wrong.

They'll come after me.

They will.

I have to believe that, and until they do, I need to stay calm and stay alive.

I follow the asshole through some marshy, wet grass to a dark building. It looks like a warehouse or big garage. I try to turn my neck to look around, see if I make out where we are, but the scary guy keeps me close to his side and moves fast. He's gripping my arm hard, but he isn't intentionally hurting me, which I hope is a good sign. Any little sign that I'm going to make it through this is a sign I'll cling to with all I've got.

The woman unlocks a door, and they bring me into an empty-looking warehouse. It's dark, but I can make out what looks like a small office. Desks and chairs sit in the corners, and shelves line one side of the space.

There's nothing to help me identify anything, and that terrifies me. This looks like a location they've prepared for this purpose. Keeping people and things out of sight.

The man turns on a few lights, but what I can see doesn't help me feel any better.

I debate yanking the duct tape off my mouth and screaming, but as I'm about to do it, the man stands in front of me and stares me down.

"You scream, I punch out your teeth. Punch. Out. Your. Teeth." He holds up the hand with all the scars on it. "We clear?" he asks and waits.

I nod.

He puts a hand against the tape over my mouth. "I'm not a nice guy," he says, "and I have no problem hitting a bitch like you."

He takes his hand away and whistles through his teeth. From an unlit corner, a dark gray dog limps forward.

He looks like a pit bull, and he's tied to a heavy collar and chain.

The man drags me over to the corner where the dog stands in a small beam of light. He kneels in front of the dog and holds his mouth open with his hands.

"The first time you scream," he says, "this happens." He holds the dog's mouth open, and I can see the dog has no teeth. None. "I take your teeth," he reminds me. "If you still think screaming is a good idea, I start with this."

He turns the dog so its flank is facing me. I can see deep, poorly healed cuts scarring the dog's back and sides. I flinch at the sight of what this poor creature's been through. More than I am worried about my own teeth, my heart breaks for this dog.

"Be like him," B says. "Be quiet. Stay on your chains. And you'll be fine."

I nod, but tears sting my eyes.

I have no doubt this guy is brutal and would hurt me if I didn't listen, but how he could keep an animal like this chained up.

It's more than I can understand. I think of my girls back home, and how I practically lose my lunch if I accidentally step on one of their paws when we're playing.

I watch the poor dog and trudge back to my dark corner of the warehouse, like an obedient, broken animal. Except I have all my teeth, and no one is going to mark up my back without a fight.

B comes up to me and yanks the tape from my mouth with one pull. "Pass code to your phone," he demands.

I tell him, and the woman unlocks my phone. She scrolls through my contacts and shakes her head. "I'm not seeing a contact number."

The guy stands beside me, his beefy hands in fists as she scrolls through my phone.

"How do you reach Tim Hawk?" she asks me.

"Tim?" I repeat. "I don't know how to reach him."

B steps closer to me. "Should we add lying to the list of things you really shouldn't do?"

I take a deep breath as the reality hits me.

Of course. This somehow has something to do with Leo's brother.

I feel so stupid.

I was out there playing private detective, when all the while, I was setting myself up as bait.

"I have never met him," I say calmly. "I moved in with his brother after Tim went missing. Nobody's heard from him in over a year."

"Let's call him," the woman suggests. "If he knows how to reach his brother, I think Leo will let us know."

She holds my phone in her lap while she punches what I assume is Leo's number into a cheap phone. Probably a burner. I pray to God that Leo answers. It's got to be late, and maybe he's already in bed. Maybe he drank himself to sleep again, or who knows what he's doing.

I hold my breath as the phone rings and rings but eventually goes to voice mail.

She hangs up and gives me a look. "He didn't answer."

B looks like he is debating how many of my teeth he can knock out with one blow.

All the fear, all the anxiety wash, over me. I'm alone with two maniacs who beat the shit out of a dog that they keep alive in this warehouse for who knows what reasons.

I mean less to them than this dog must. If I don't give them what they want, I'm sure they'll make good on their threats. But I can guess they won't keep me chained up in this warehouse forever.

"I'm going to be sick," I say.

There's nothing else I can do. I didn't eat dinner, and all the fear and the beer in my belly mix together and revolt. I turn my head away from B and empty the contents on my stomach onto the concrete floor.

"Goddamn it." B seems inconvenienced but not surprised. He gives the woman a look. "Get her some water." He grabs a fistful of rags from a shelf and throws them at me. "Clean that up." He kicks a plastic bucket my way. "Use that if you're going to do that shit again."

I take the rags as best I can with my hands bound, cleaning the floor before I dab my mouth with the end of my shirt. I want to cry, but I won't. I won't let them see me any more vulnerable than I already am.

I shiver, suddenly cold.

I slide down to sit on the floor and tremble, trying to control my breathing.

Remain calm.

The woman returns with a bottle of water in her hands. She glares at me before she untwists the cap and holds the bottle out to me. "Don't be stupid," she warns.

I shake my head, and my instinct is to say thank you for the water, but I don't.

Fuck these two.

I'm not going to thank them for anything.

I take a sip of the water, and before I even taste it, the cool sensation on my mouth feels so good, I suck down several large sips before I register that the water tastes funny. I stop drinking, thinking maybe it tastes weird because I puked, and take another mouthful, swishing it around to get rid of the odd flavor.

"You want me to call him back?" the woman asks.

The man nods but doesn't say anything.

I silently pray that Leo answers the phone.

Maybe he'll think it's Tim calling. Maybe he won't care but will get pissed off enough to answer.

All I can do is wait and pray.

I watch as she dials the number again, but when her face falls, I can tell it's gone to voice mail again.

"Send a text?" she asks. "Can't hurt."

"Hold off," B says.

I gulp down almost the entire bottle, trying not to lose my shit.

My fingertips feel numb, and there's a light sensation in my body like I'm both heavy and weightless at the same time.

I've been drugged. I know I have. My body doesn't feel right at all.

I panic, dropping the water bottle on the ground. It falls with a dull thud against the concrete, and the last of the contents spill out on the floor. I try to stick my fingers into my mouth to make myself sick, but B holds his fist in the air, and I stop.

I'm too weak to think through my options.

I'm too tired to even feel fear. Maybe that's a good thing.

Images swim in front of my eyes, the colors muted and dark but so real.

I see Josh at Checkers, the fabric of his shirt against my cheek as we danced. I see the dog in the corner, straining silently against his chains.

And then Leo. Leo's here.

In front of my eyes, at least, the scruff of his beard under my hands as I hold his face close to mine.

"Leo," I gasp. "I love you." And everything goes dark.

12

LEO

WHEN I PULL up to my house and see Arrow's truck, the first thing I do is take a huge breath. I'm ready to fight for Lia, whatever it takes, but I'm not about to pull another man out of her bed.

But it doesn't look like I'm going to have to. As soon as I punch the clicker to open my garage door, Josh is climbing out of his truck.

"Hey," he says. He looks as pissed as I feel. "Where's Lia?"

"Lia?" I'm not following. "Out with you. Date not end so great? She ditch your ass?" I want to chuckle but hold it back.

Serves the fucker right.

Arrow shakes his head. "Something's wrong. We went to Checkers, just like we planned. Lia went

185

CHELLE BLISS

into the bathroom and didn't come out. After like twenty minutes, I had a bartender check on her, but she was gone." He steps a little too close to me and demands answers. "What the fuck are you two up to? Do you think this is a game?"

"Up to?" I'm genuinely stunned. But my shock comes out hard and fast as anger. I grab Arrow by the front of the shirt and shove him hard against the side of his truck. "What the fuck are you talking about?" I demand, shaking him. "We're not up to anything. You took my goddamn roommate to a bar on a date!"

Arrow tenses his biceps, but he doesn't make a move to shove me away. "Didn't Lia tell you the plan? This wasn't a date, you asshole."

My stomach sinks.

She'd wanted to talk to me all day.

I ignored her.

"I have no fucking idea what you're talking about," I admit, the fear clawing its way up my back. I release Arrow and scrub my face with my hands. "Back the fuck up. What happened?"

Arrow now looks genuinely worried. "We've got to go inside. We need to see if Lia's home."

I rush past him and into the open garage. I shove open the interior door, calling her name.

"Lia! Lia!" I storm into the living room. The lights are off, the way I left them.

Josh follows behind me. "Lia!" he shouts.

I give him a shit look. I can hear Lia's dogs barking upstairs, going crazy. They are still in her bedroom.

"I'm going to check her room." I point at him. "You stay down here."

I flick on every light as I head through the house toward the stairs.

I don't trust Arrow, and I sure as fuck don't want him upstairs. I don't know what he wants or what he's doing, but if Lia's up in her room, the last thing I want is for them to have some kind of sweet reunion in front of me.

I storm up the stairs and knock on Lia's door. The dogs are panting and clawing at it, but I don't hear any sign that Lia's inside.

I push the door open, and the lights are off, but the noise-canceling sound machine and night-light she leaves on for the dogs when she leaves them home alone are still running.

The dogs spill out past me and race down the stairs. I follow behind them and grab Arrow again when I find him in the living room, pacing.

"What the fuck is going on?" I demand. "Where is she?"

"We need to find her," he says, his voice quiet. "We need to call the police."

"The cops? What the fuck? Why?" I shove him away from me. "Tell me what the fuck happened tonight!"

Arrow picks up his phone and checks it. "I'll tell you everything," he says. "But has she called or texted you? Have you heard from her at all in the last hour?"

I reach into the front pocket of my vest and pull out my phone. I haven't even checked it since I silenced it at Morris's house.

"Holy fuck," I say as I scan the screen. There are three calls from the same unknown number and one text from Lia. "She texted," I say, relief flooding my gut.

"What'd she say?" Arrow asks. He comes close to look over my shoulder, but I move away from him so I can read the text.

As the words register, I feel sick. An icy feeling spreads through my veins, and I want to punch someone, anyone. But the first person I see is Arrow.

I drop my phone and throw a punch at his chin,

but he ducks enough that I only graze his jaw.

"Stop, you stupid motherfucker. Stop!" Josh holds his chin with his hand but keeps the other hand in front of him, pushing me away from him. "What did she say in the text? What does it say?"

"It's not from her," I grit out and hand him my phone as I sink onto the couch.

Lia: If you want your girl back, give us Tim.

Arrow reads the text aloud and lets a string of curses fly. "Text them back," he says.

"What? Fuck no." I grab my phone away from him. "Tell me what the fuck you got Lia into!"

I've had enough. I leap toward Arrow, ready to smash his shitty face in, but he blocks me and shoves me back against the couch.

"You want to waste time beating my ass while somebody's got Lia, or do you want to sit the fuck down and listen!" he roars.

"I really want to beat your face in," I seethe. "And I will. You mark my fucking words. If any harm comes to Lia, I'll beat you within an inch of your worthless life."

"I'd like to see you try, you little shit." As soon as he says the words, Arrow holds up a hand. "Fuck. Forget it, okay? Let it go. Let's focus on Lia."

He paces a few steps away from me, probably

trying to get his wits together like I am. Pixie has come up to my ankles and is whining, rubbing her face against me. I pick her up because I know I can't kill Arrow with a tiny trembling dog in my hands. And right now, I need him alive and conscious to tell me everything he knows.

"Start at the beginning," I demand.

Josh glares at me. "What did Lia tell you? About her plan, about our talk this morning."

I scowl at him. "Why don't you do what I fucking asked and start at the beginning?" I don't want to admit to him that I didn't listen to her. That she tried to talk to me, told me she'd done some research and had news. I couldn't give her five minutes to listen.

Arrow flares his nostrils but starts talking. "Lia called. Asked me to meet her at her store. Confronted me about the house this morning."

As soon as he says the words, I feel like the biggest piece of shit on this goddamn planet...again.

"She wanted me to know that she did some research, and she knew that I couldn't just kick you out of here in two weeks, even if Tim didn't show for his court date."

Now that's news I would have wanted to hear.

No wonder Lia was all bright and worked up this morning.

God fucking damn me and my stupidity.

"She told me she knew the whole process could take months. The court would give Tim extra time, and that basically the best outcome for all of us would be for us to work together to find Tim."

I nod.

She would come up with a plan like that. Everyone working together. She teamed up with my nemesis to help me and put herself in harm's way doing it. Meanwhile, I was debating cutting and running. Hitting the road and abandoning her and everything I have. I was so close to leaving this whole town, my house, my business, in the rearview. The entire time, Lia was out on some mission to find my brother with Arrow.

"So, what the fuck happened?" I demand.

"We went to Checkers. Figured that if Tim and his wife really were hanging out there, they'd recognize you, if they hadn't already."

Damn. That's why she went with him tonight. A date that probably wasn't even a date. Not a real one, at least.

"What happened at the bar?" I ask, my mind spinning.

"We had a couple drinks, danced…" He stops for a second and goes on. "She used the bathroom and took a long time. When she didn't come out after like twenty minutes…"

"Twenty fucking minutes?" I demand. "Why the hell would you wait twenty minutes before making sure she was okay?"

Arrow hardened his face. "I—we almost kissed. It didn't happen, she stopped it, and I thought maybe she was mad or confused. I don't know. Splashing cold water on her face, calling you…" He gave me a look. "I think she's really into you, but there's no denying we have some wicked chemistry. I honestly thought she was trying to figure out what she wanted. Me or you."

That gutted me.

"I let it go longer than I should have, and I'm fucking kicking myself over it now," he admits. "The bartender went in, said there was no sign of Lia. At first, I got pissed. I thought maybe you and she were playing me somehow, but that didn't make sense. I came back here, figuring you'd come and picked her up and I'd find her safe at home, laughing at me with you."

I cringe and swallow a hint of bile that's creeping up my throat. "She's not here." I'm stating the obvious, but my mind is swirling, and I can't stop the words from coming out. "I didn't know what she was doing. I didn't talk to her all day."

"All day?" he echoes. "Why not?"

"Doesn't matter now," I say. "She's not with you, she's not here, but she's with someone."

I think back over everything Arrow said. He tried to kiss her, but she didn't want it. She didn't want him. Maybe, just maybe, that's because she still wants me.

I grab my phone and show Arrow the missed calls. "You know this number?"

He types the area code into his contacts list, searching for a match, but comes up empty. He shakes his head. "Burner, I'm going to guess."

They want Tim.

They have Lia.

"Who are they?" I ask. "Who would want to get to Tim?" I look at him with fresh suspicion. "Is this you?" I demand. "Is this some game to flush out my brother?"

"No, Leo. Before you go there—Jesus. No." Arrow looks at me and throws his hands in the air. "I swear to God, man. I have nothing to do with this. I had no idea this could happen. I would never have brought Lia out tonight if I'd had any idea she might have been in some kind of danger."

"Think," I demand. "You know these low-life scumbags. This is what you do!"

Josh clenches his hands into fists. "I know you're fucking pissed right now, but I think the sooner we stop fighting and start working together, the sooner we'll find Lia."

I don't want to trust him, but he has a point. If I'd stopped and fucking listened to Lia this morning, maybe I could have stopped this whole thing from happening.

Working together is exactly what we should have been doing all day. But I was too pigheaded, organizing a pity party for one, to listen to anyone else's good ideas.

I don't trust Arrow and I'm not about to call him a friend, but I'm willing to call a truce if it means finding Lia faster.

"All right," I say. "What do we do? Call the cops? Report her missing?"

"Maybe..." Arrow is pacing, thinking.

I set Pixie down on the couch and pace my own route across the carpet.

"They want Tim," he says, thinking out loud. "So that leaves us two possibilities. The first is that you and I aren't the only ones Tim's fucked over. The second is that Tim himself is behind this."

"What?" That throws me sideways. "How the fuck would he be behind this?"

"I don't know, Leo." Arrow seems as stuck as I feel. "Think about it, though. He knows I'm hot on his heels, and if he's keeping tabs on you and this house, he knows that you know. Maybe this is some harebrained junkie plot to find out whether we actually do know where he is."

That gives me a glimmer of hope.

I know my brother.

He may be an addict, he may be a deadbeat, but I know in my soul he'd never hurt another person. He wouldn't harm a hair on Lia's head.

"Could it be Tim?" I ask. "How do we know?"

"We text them back," Arrow says. "You tell them, whoever they are, you don't know where your brother is. You haven't talked to him. Tell them that if they know, you'd really love to get in touch with him because he's fucking you in the ass too."

I punch a message back, but before I hit send, I look at him. "What if this isn't Tim?" I have to consider it. "If Tim is in some kind of trouble with somebody else, if they hear we don't have any idea how to find him, what's gonna happen to Lia?"

Josh nods and holds up his hand. "Right. It could go either way. Could be Tim, or it could be…"

"It could be anyone. And I'm not taking a chance with Lia's life." I delete the message, so I don't accidentally send it. "What the fuck do we do?"

Arrow points at the phone. "Ask them. Ask them what they want from Tim. Let's play a little ball."

That seems safe enough. If they think we know where Tim is, they'll keep the conversation going. Maybe. If it is Tim, he'll definitely keep talking to find out what exactly we do or don't know about him.

"Should I call the number or text back?"

"Try calling," Josh says.

I pull up the list of missed calls and select the unknown number. I hit redial and wait. The phone rings once, twice, and a third time before the call is picked up and disconnected.

"No voice mail," I report. "Sounded like someone answered but hung up."

"Did you hear anything?" he asks.

I shake my head.

"Send a text," he says. "Just ask who they are

and what they want. Keep it simple, and don't give anything away."

I don't know what the fuck I'm going to give away in a text, but I follow his lead.

Me: Who is this? What do you want?

We both watch my phone. I unsilence it in case they call back.

The severity of the situation hits me, and my rage morphs into something like terror. I can't imagine calling the cops to report her missing. That would mean she's really gone. Really in danger. That I might never see her again.

The fact that Lia may be alone, scared, in danger someplace because of me, because of my chickenshit decisions…I want to scream or punch something, someone.

"What now?" I ask Arrow, desperation making me crazy. "Call the cops? Report Lia missing? Kidnapped? Maybe I should go to the shop. Check there. She could be anywhere, maybe she's…"

"Leo." Josh holds up a hand. "There will be plenty of time to start searching. Let's see if they respond. Okay? There's still a chance this is Tim trying to find out what we know."

I'm not holding my breath waiting for that text.

Josh and I watch my phone until finally, a text pops back up.

We'll trade Tim for Lia. You have twenty-four hours. We'll contact you with a time and location.

"What do you think?" I ask. "Is it Tim? Is he behind this?"

Arrow shakes his head. "I mean…it could be. There's no way to know."

"Let's play this out," I say. "If it is Tim, he's given us twenty-four hours to prove whether or not we know how to reach him."

Arrow nods. "If we contact him, he may let Lia go and run. If we don't contact him, best-case is he knows we can't, and he leaves Lia for us to pick up where he tells us he left her." He looks at me. "I can't imagine he wants to add kidnapping and who knows what else to his list of charges."

I hope to hell that's true. "And if it's not Tim?" I ask.

Arrow doesn't answer.

"We have twenty-four hours to find him," I say. I grab my phone and prepare to start dialing.

"Who are you calling? Are you calling the cops?" Arrow asks. "We need to be careful, Leo. We need to work as a team on this. Lia's life could be in danger."

"I know that," I say.

That's why I'm not going to the cops. Not just yet. Like anyone would when they're in trouble, I go to family first.

But not my family.

I pick up the phone and call the one man who might kill me whether or not we find Lia and get her back safe.

I call Tiny.

13

LIA

I SEE LEO'S FACE. He's far away, and he looks so, so angry. It has to be about Josh. He knows we slow danced. He knows we almost kissed.

I want to explain to him what happened. That I only went there with Josh to try to help. To save the house. But Leo won't listen. He's angry, and he's pulling away.

He's leaving. For a minute, I want to cry.

Leo isn't only leaving.

He's leaving me.

He's walking away from everything.

The house, the business.

I watch him go.

He climbs on his bike and rides away. I'm standing in the driveway of the house looking after him, and a storm rolls in. I feel cold now, the chill seeping down to my bones.

"Leo," I call out. I want to call after him, but everything I say sounds like I'm crying. I can't make his name sound right. It sounds like I have cotton in my mouth, and my tongue is sticking to the roof of it every time I try to call out to him.

Before I know what's happening, he's pulled away and I'm alone, standing in Leo's garage. I smell smoke, but I can't find where it's coming from. My first thought goes to my dogs, and I try to pry my eyes open so I can run to them. My girls could be in trouble, but somehow, I can't manage to open my eyes.

I'm floating somewhere between sleep and being awake. I can hear sounds around me, but I don't know what I'm hearing. I'm not sure where I am. I only know I'm cold, so cold. But when I try to cover up, there's nothing there.

I roll onto my side and try to stretch, but I can't move my hands. The smell of smoke sends my heart into a panic, and I kick my feet, my high-heeled sandals scraping across a hard, cold surface.

I crack my eyes open, and through the blurry haze, I see the ember of a cigarette being smoked far in the distance.

"You think we should feed her?" It's that skanky woman from the bar.

The fog dissipates, and I remember the threats.

The dog with no teeth.

"Fuck her," the guy says. "She'll be fine for a day."

I shift onto my back, and everything—and I mean everything—hurts. I must have passed out on my shoulder, and with my hands bound, I can't straighten out. But I lie flat and try to take deep breaths. The scent of smoke hits me like a ton of bricks, and I manage to roll over and hit the bucket before I throw up again.

There's nothing in my stomach other than a little water, but my body doesn't seem to get it. I heave and cough, crouching over the bucket until my body gives up.

"I need to pee," I plead.

"So, go." The man called B nods toward the bucket. "No point in being modest after all that." He waves a disgusted hand toward the bucket.

I want to tell him to go fuck himself, but I hold up my hands. "I would, but someone's going to have to help me." I narrow my eyes at him. "Not you. Her."

I'll play their little game for now. I'm too weak

to try to attack her if she does come close enough to help me pee. I remember his warning about punching out my teeth.

"Please," I beg nicely. "I'm dehydrated, and unless you want me to piss all over myself…"

They trade looks and the skanky woman comes over to me. She grimaces when she sees the watery puke in the bucket and looks away.

"I'm going to help you stand," she says. "Your shit's practically hanging out of those shorts. You can just pull them to one side and piss in the bucket."

Damn.

On the one hand, I'm relieved because I wouldn't relish having my pants off and being even more vulnerable in front of these two.

The woman grabs my bicep and helps me to stand. I spread my legs over the bucket and turn my head to her. "Some toilet paper?" I ask.

"Jesus Christ, would you piss already?" The guy flicks his cigarette at the dog, who whimpers quietly in his dark corner.

The woman hands me a single paper towel, one of those rough, commercial-folded ones. Whatever. It isn't soft, but it will dry me off and keep my shorts from getting wet.

I pee in the bucket, for once thankful that I'd traveled in my van for so many months without access to a toilet or sink. I've mastered peeing in places that would make the average woman miserable.

Once I am done, I lean my back against the cold, hard wall and slide carefully down to my ass so I can sit.

"Can I get some bread or crackers? Anything to eat?" I know they already said they weren't going to feed me, but maybe my persistence would change their minds. "And I wouldn't mind some undrugged water."

B looks as if he wants to punch my teeth out there and then, but the woman looks to him.

"Can't hurt," she says. "I have some crackers in the desk. Maybe it'll stop her from puking."

The man shrugs and looks away while the woman yanks open a drawer and pulls out a sleeve of crackers. They are open and the end hasn't been twisted closed, so they are probably stale as hell, but I don't care. Anything to take the taste of sick off my tongue.

She slides the crackers across the concrete toward me, but they don't quite reach me, so I struggle onto my knees and crawl over to reach them.

"Thank you for these," I say.

The woman doesn't respond but rolls a bottle of water my way. It isn't cold, but it is unopened, so I trust it isn't drugged.

The restraints on my wrists are loose enough that I can eat a few crackers and drink some water.

The good thing about snacking is B and the female captor are talking and ignoring me as I listen to every word carefully.

"I can't sit here all day and babysit this bitch," the woman says.

"Go home. What the fuck do I care," the guy replies.

"What are you going to do with her?" she asks.

He glares at me, and I lower my eyes. "She's going to sit there and keep her mouth shut." He cracks his knuckles loudly, reminding me of his earlier promise. "And I won't have to do a goddamn thing."

"Are you going to leave her alone?" the woman asks.

It sounds like she's concerned what he might do with me, or to me, if we are alone.

I am concerned about that too.

The terrifying man stands up from the desk he's been sitting on, and he walks over to me. He sets a roll of paper towels beside my bucket, along with another full bottle of water.

He crouches down beside me. His face is level with mine, and I look away so I won't have to smell his breath.

"I'm going to show you a little trick," he says.

He points with a finger to the ceiling of the warehouse. In every corner, cameras are mounted, pointing at various angles across the space. He swipes at his cell phone and opens up an app. I can see on the display a really high-quality image of the warehouse. I can see him, me, and the woman as though I am looking in a mirror and not at a camera feed.

"You make a sound, I'll know," he says. "You move, I'll know. You scream for help, you try to leave, you do anything but piss, sleep, and drink your water, I'll know."

I nod. "I'll be quiet."

"We made contact with your dumb-ass boyfriend," he tells me. "We've arranged a trade. So, don't do anything stupid, and you'll be back home safe by midnight."

"Really?" I can't even hope what he's saying is true.

"I'd show you, but we turned your phone off. No need to make it easy on the cops or your friends to find you. If they come through with their half of the deal, you'll get your phone, and you can go home and forget any of this ever happened."

Tears sting my eyes at the hope that what he's saying is true.

"But wait," he says, taking on a sick, game show host voice. "There's more. Watch and wait."

The woman starts to chuckle as if she knows what's coming.

He stands up and walks out of the warehouse altogether. I don't hear any doors slam, so I don't know where he is, but a minute later, I hear his voice coming from some kind of sound system.

"Mikey," he calls out, his voice echoing through the empty warehouse. "Attack!"

At that, the dog on the chain immediately responds. The scarred, toothless barrel of a dog is snarling, barking like a hound out of hell, pulling at the chain that's attached to his collar like he'll kill anything and anyone in sight.

I'm not sure what good a toothless attack dog is going to do, but the point is made. They've got me.

They have the means to scare me and even hurt me.

"I get it," I say quietly. "I won't give you any trouble."

"It's just a couple hours now," the woman says, but there's no sweetness in her voice.

To my shock, my kidnappers leave me alone in the warehouse. Before they pull away, I hear through the speakers, "Remember, we can see and hear you."

As if I could forget.

As soon as they are gone, I lie back down on the floor. I use the roll of paper towels as a pillow, and I sob. Tears coat my face, and I pray harder than I've ever prayed before.

What if Josh thinks I ran out on our date? It would have been a shitty thing to do, but what if he thought I got cold feet or something and left him instead of leaving to go to the bathroom?

What if no one knows I'm missing?

No. Those people told me they reached out to my…boyfriend.

The tears flow harder as I realize that my boyfriend could be Josh or Leo. I have them both in my phone, but I was planning a hot date last night with Josh.

I'm so stupid.

I should have stayed home.

Talked to Leo.

Gone to my dad.

By now, we might have figured out a plan to save Leo's house. We could have hired a private investigator to find Tim and Juliette.

So many could-haves. But I had to butt my big booty into the mix and follow my hormones instead of my better judgment.

I turn my head, and I see Mikey, the chained-up dog, lying with his chin against the concrete.

"Mikey?" I say his name really quietly, hoping the speakers won't pick up my voice.

The dog's ears perk up a bit, and his tail flops hard against the concrete in a single, cautious wag.

My heart melts into a million pieces.

"Are you hungry, baby?" I ask.

I pull a cracker out of the sleeve and peek up at the cameras. If I don't move from my lying-down position, I can probably slide the cracker close enough for him to get it. I try with the first one, but it doesn't quite reach far enough.

Mikey looks at it curiously, his tail whomping against the floor.

"I'll try again. Watch," I tell him, still whispering.

It's no easy feat getting him a cracker with my hands bound, but I end up flicking the cracker with my fingers like I'm playing a game of table football. The cracker is stale enough that it doesn't crumble but skids across the floor close enough for Mikey to snap it up between his gums.

"Might be tastier if you had teeth, but most dogs don't really chew anyway."

Mikey starts creeping closer to me. His belly is flat against the concrete, and he's doing this frog-like army crawl to get closer.

How could these monsters keep this dog chained up?

"When was the last time you saw the outside, boy?" I ask. "You want another cracker?"

Mikey is panting now, and it's impossible not to see his toothless mouth as anything but adorable.

I slide another cracker over, and Mikey wiggles his way as far as the chain can reach. I scoot slightly closer to him. I move the roll of paper towels with me, so that if they are checking the cameras, they will see me in the same position I've been in.

And hopefully they won't notice that I've shifted.

Once I'm close enough to Mikey to feed him, I give him crackers from my hand, one after another until the sleeve is gone.

"I'll probably regret that," I whisper. "I'm going to get hungry at some point."

I sit up and unscrew the top from my water bottle. I take a sip and wait, hoping that if my movement sets off the cameras, they'll think I'm drinking water.

When nothing happens, I pour a little water in my hand and carefully hold it out to Mikey. The doggie doesn't hesitate for even a second. He laps up the water like he's dying of thirst. He probably is.

I give him the rest of the water in the first bottle those assholes left for me.

"We'd better pace ourselves," I whisper. "We only have this one other bottle, and it has to last us."

I have no idea how long I'll be here alone. There is nothing I can do except lie here, waiting. If I try to leave, they'll come back, and who knows whether they'll be armed or what. If I make too much noise, try to escape, anything...

If there were no cameras, I'd take my chances,

but they showed me the cameras were there for a reason. They want me to know they're in control.

I'm stunned out of my mind when I feel a hot blast of breath against my leg. Mickey has snuggled up beside me. He's lying on his belly, his chin on the floor, but his warmth seeps through and warms my cold body.

I can't snuggle him with my arms bound, but I curl up as close to him as I can for warmth.

As I start to cry again, I pray to God, Leo, and everyone I've ever loved. "We're going to make it, Mikey. We're going to be okay."

14

LEO

I LOOK AT JOSH. He's still pacing my living room. We need to make a plan, and that plan will involve all hands on deck, but that doesn't mean telling Tiny is going to be easy.

I may not have to worry about what happens to my house after breaking the news to him that his daughter has been kidnapped.

"You may want to call a priest while I call Lia's dad," I mutter.

"Why?" Josh looks confused.

"Cuz Tiny's going to fucking kill me, man." I don't care that it's nearly midnight now. I dial Tiny's number, and he answers on the third ring.

"What," he grates out. "Fuck me. What time is it? This better be damn important."

I take a deep breath and break the news as calmly as I can, then I listen, waiting for Tiny to blister my ear.

He doesn't, but he says, "I'll deal with you in person. On my way. Don't fucking move."

Over the next forty-five minutes, Dog and Morris show up at my house. Josh is drinking coffee, while my rage is more than enough to keep me wide awake and sharp.

"Fire up another pot," Dog says. "I take mine with sugar."

I head into the kitchen with Morris hot on my heels.

"We're going to have problems with Tiny," Morris warns.

"No shit." I'm not trying to be disrespectful. I'm resigned to it. Just when I started thinking that there could be more there with Lia, that there's something between us worth fighting for.

I can't wait to see how supportive Tiny's going to be of his prospect dating his little girl now.

"I feel sick about this, Morris. I had no fucking clue this could happen."

I toss the filter in the trash and make the biggest pot of coffee the machine can brew.

"I'm just saying. Nothing about Tiny is small.

Especially his temper." Morris is pale. He's wearing the same wrinkled T-shirt he had on when I left his house earlier, but he looks like he's aged years in the hours since I last saw him.

"I'm prepared for that," I say. "Whatever the consequences." Saying it out loud actually makes what's about to happen easier to take.

If Tiny didn't want his daughter dating a biker before—specifically me—then a guy whose family shit got his daughter taken by kidnappers and held for ransom, is definitely out of the question.

Any hope I had for that possibility of more with Lia...up in flames.

A pounding at the door sets the dogs barking and my teeth on edge. "Time to face the firing squad," I say.

I open the door, but before it's even open three inches, Tiny's boot kicks it back so hard it hits the wall with a bang. He lunges forward with his hands outstretched.

"I'm gonna kill you!"

Dog is up in a flash, and he and Morris stand on either side of the big guy, holding him back by the shoulders.

I wave the guys off. "It's all right," I tell them. "I can take it."

215

Morris and Dog back off, but Josh rises to join me.

"Sir," he says, "I'm Josh Aronowicz. It's my fault that Lia is in this situation. If there's anyone who needs a beating, it's me, not Leo."

I frown at Arrow for standing up for me. I don't know what game he's playing, but I don't need his help. Turns out, Tiny doesn't seem to care who's to blame. He wants to take his anger out on all of us.

"You dumb-ass pieces of crime-playing shit!" Tiny swears and curses, kicking a path through my living room that the carpet's gonna be feeling for a long time. "You!" He points at Arrow. "I don't give a shit about you, this bail business, or your weak-ass apologies. All I want to know is how someone was able to *kidnap my daughter* while she was out with you."

He turns and thrusts a meaty paw at me. "This one over here isn't much better, but at least she's lived with him for a year, and he's managed not to get her ass kidnapped."

I watch, a little bit stunned by what's happening. Is Tiny defending me?

I'm not letting it go to my head.

"You're a bail agent who not only lost his felon, but you endangered the lives of innocent people."

Tiny shakes his head. "I damn well hope you'll be considering another line of work after this."

Arrow looks like he's being called out by his grandma for masturbating at the dining table.

"And you." Tiny looks at me. "If I find out that anyone, and I mean anyone, has laid a hand on my daughter…" He shudders. "I will go to prison for killing you," he said. "And I will enjoy every minute of it."

He spends a few more minutes explaining how he's going bury my remains and piss on my poorly hidden grave before Dog steps in with a helping hand. "Okay," he says. "Now that we're clear how many different ways you're planning to kill these two, let's figure out a plan."

Morris nods and hands Tiny a huge mug of coffee. "We know these assholes want Tim or these assholes *are* Tim. When did you last hear from this jailbird, and what can we do to find him?" He directs the question to both Arrow and me.

We jump in with what we know. We talk about the timeline, when I last heard from my brother, and we go over everything that Arrow knows about Tim and Juliette.

But like everything else, rehashing the details brings us right back to where we started.

No new information.

No ideas.

No leads.

Tiny looks at Arrow and points to a chair.

Arrow looks as if he's considering not sitting, sizing up Tiny, the vibe in the room, and the bikers who outnumber him, but he drops down.

"I wanna know everything," Tiny seethes. "Leave no detail out."

I'm not sure I want to hear every detail again, but if there's any nugget, any shred of information that might shed new light on what happened, I'll listen to Arrow describe in detail almost kissing my girl. Thankfully, he leaves that part out.

He explains that they were dancing, she went to the bathroom, that he thought there might be some confusion over whether or not this was a date, and that for a while, even he wasn't sure if Lia and I were trying to pull something over on him.

"Sweet fuck," Tiny blurts out. "You all need to lay off the podcasts or whatever shit you watch."

I don't bother correcting him.

We talk through the fact that the solution has to lie some place in or around Checkers.

"We need someone on the inside at Checkers to talk," Tiny says. "There's no way a kidnapping happens inside a bar without somebody seeing something. Somebody knows Tim or you—" He points accusingly at Arrow. "And they knew something was up when you came in two nights in a row, feeling people out."

Even Dog shakes his head at that. "Isn't there some kind of bounty hunter code? Do you have, like, other shithead friends you can ask around? How easy can it be for a felon on the run with a woman to stay in hiding? No money, no friends." He looks at me. "You haven't heard from your brother, so you're not helping him out."

It wasn't a question, but I feel the need to answer it anyway. Not if there's even a suggestion out there that I might be helping out Tim.

"Hell no," I say. "It's been a year plus, and after everything I've learned about him this week...that asshole better know not to come to me for help."

Tiny's looking furious and exhausted—a dangerous combination for all of us. He wants someone to blame—we all do. But even more than that, I want answers. I want to *do* something. Unlike before, when I wanted to run away from this, I now want names, addresses, and goddamn phone numbers. I want to kick ass with my own hands and bring Lia back home safely.

"Checkers," I say. "We have to get back in there and shake them down. If they know a girl was kidnapped, I can't imagine any of them want to take the fall for that kind of shit."

"Those people," Josh adds, "they don't talk. Or they won't now. That's why I was trying to hang out, see what I could shake loose. This isn't my first fucking rodeo. In my line of work, you don't get clients by having a slick Instagram account. You've got to hang out where the clients are. Let them know who you are and build up that trust."

"Trust," Tiny spits. "You of all people should know there's no fucking honor among thieves."

Josh continues, but the tension is building. We're all feeling the pressure of decisions made when we had no clue how high the stakes really were.

"Exactly my point," Arrow says. "It cuts both ways. If I'm gonna do what I do, people have to know who I am. I'm guessing that bringing Lia there made people suspicious. And yeah... That's on me."

"One hundred percent," Tiny says, glaring at Arrow. "Which is why you're going there tomorrow, and you're going to talk to every single person who works there, owns the place, the suppliers of the beer. I don't care what you have to do, someone in that bar knows how to find Tim. You find these people. No more of this James Bond bullshit. You go in heavy and hard," Tiny demands. "You carry?"

Josh shakes his head. "No, I—"

Tiny holds up a hand. "I don't want to hear it." He looks at Dog. "You help this pansy-ass bail whatever he is. You don't take no for an answer, you hear me? You shake loose everyone and everything you can, and don't give up until we get a lead on my daughter."

Dog nods and pats his belt. "We'll get lips flapping, Tiny. We'll get something."

After arguing for what seems like hours, disagreeing about everything, finally, Tiny pulls rank. "I'm in charge from here on out." Since he's the president of the MC, none of us are going to fight him. He eyeballs Arrow. "You got a problem with that, you can go. We take care of our own, and right now, there's only one man in this room who's not one of us."

I swallow a mouthful of sand as he says that. Tiny's supporting me, but only because he has to. And if this thing doesn't end well with Lia...I'll be the first one to pay the price, and I'll take that punishment willingly.

CHELLE BLISS

"Priority one is finding Tim," Tiny says as he points to Josh and then Dog. "You cover Checkers. You got that? I'm putting every member of the club on this," Tiny continues. "By noon tomorrow, I want a lead on this Tim person."

Josh opens his mouth to say something, but Dog shakes his head and pulls Arrow back.

"When Tiny gives an order, you nod your head. If you want it to stay on your neck," Dog says. He points to Arrow. "You hear anything from anyone about anything that could help find Lia, you tell us, all of us, immediately. You hear?"

Arrow nods. "Look, I want to find Lia as much as—"

Tiny looks at Arrow with a withering look. "Don't make me kick your ass. I'm old, I'm tired, and—" he cracks his knuckles for dramatic effect "—I'm out of patience."

Arrow nods, and he and Dog depart.

That leaves Morris, Tiny, and me.

I can't say anything. I can't apologize, can't defend myself. All I do is sit there. Miserable.

I stare at my coffee, all lukewarm and gross in the bottom of my mug. I can't even imagine where Lia is right now. How scared or cold or hungry she might be. I can't even begin to think what

222

she's going through if whoever has her wants her hurt or scared. I'm hoping if they really want to trade her for Tim, that they won't actually hurt her. But if they do... This is the one time I wish I had weapons. But it's also probably for the best I don't.

Tiny and Dog have an arsenal of guns, but Morris stopped carrying a long time ago. But those guys, they'll go in dirty if they think they have to. I probably should have patted down Tiny's pockets when he got here. No doubt he's got a couple bullets with my name on them.

"Where you want me?" Morris asks.

"Go home to your family," Tiny says. "If we don't have any information by morning, we may need to start calling in favors. I'll be calling on you for that."

I knew what he meant. I'd never met them, but I knew they had connections in all kinds of places—law enforcement, private security. You don't trot out those kinds of friends unless you need a serious favor—the kind that's not easy to pay back.

I can't believe my brother put me and everyone I care about in this situation. I feel sick, ashamed. I want this nightmare to end for Lia, but goddamn, I want this to be over for all of us. Ever since Tim walked out, my life has been one shame-filled shit sandwich. I've been taking bites of it one at a time.

Morris comes over and squeezes my shoulder with one hand. "Stay strong," he says. I know he means the squeeze to be helpful, but I can't take any comfort in it. It reminds me of how much I stand to lose. The people I've come to rely on, treat as family. Alice and Morris and Zoey think of Lia as family.

What the fuck will they do if something happens to her?

I don't see any outcome that is recoverable except one—finding Lia and bringing her home safe.

Morris and Tiny trade looks, and I swear they communicate on some subconscious level. Morris nods as if he's agreed to some silent plan between the two of them.

Whatever they say, whatever they want to do, I'll do it. I can't stand the thought that Lia is spending a night alone someplace. Not knowing if she's being harmed or if she's cold or hungry fucking kills me.

I hope to God my brother has her, because as much as I want to kill him for what he's doing to all of us, I'd rather her be with someone who I know is a fuck-up but harmless.

After Morris leaves, it's just me and Tiny and the worst night of my life. And it's only getting started.

"You wanna crash here?" I ask. "I think it'll be good for you to be here in case Lia comes back. Just in case anything goes down here at the house."

"Where you planning on going?" Tiny's eyes are red, and he's looking at me with distrust. Even through the stress, I can tell he's beat.

We all are.

"I'm going to go look for her, man," I say. "I need to be out there. Looking."

Tiny shakes his head. "Where the fuck you gonna look? If you have any idea where she might be, your ass should have already been there. Let the guys handle it."

I tear at my hair with my hands. "I can't stand by and do nothing."

"I want you to not go off half-cocked, driving the streets in the middle of the night like an asshole," he says. "We don't need you in trouble too."

"Come on, man," I punch the table, bringing the dogs running for cover.

Tiny scowls. "I'm gonna get my ass back to the compound."

"You should be here. This is her home. Why don't you take the dogs and go on up and get a little rest? An hour, tops. I'll wake you up if anything happens."

Tiny grunts. "If I crash for an hour, will you keep your puny ass here and not go riding off into the night to look for her?"

"Yeah," I lie. "You rest for one hour, I'll chill the fuck out and think about everything I can do to find Tim, and we'll regroup."

He seems a lot more vulnerable now. Lost. Like all the anger and rage have been hiding a confused, sad man. And the truth is, this is exhausting. Scary.

He's only just got Lia back, and I'm sure he's realizing how deep his feelings for her run. He may not have memories of holding her through skinned knees and graduations, but Lia leaves a deep impression. To know her is to be struck by her light. Her kindness. I can't imagine finding that woman as an adult, learning she was my daughter, only to be faced with possibly losing her.

I can't fathom having her and losing her either. I told myself it was all fun and games. Light. Easy.

Fuck easy. I'll never, ever take what I have for

granted again. Not my business, my house. My friends. My family.

"I won't sleep," Tiny says. But I can tell he's considering it. "Is it weird sleeping in my grown-up kid's bed?"

"Nah," I say. "It's not weird." I immediately picture the lube and condoms. Fuck, I haven't been in her room since yesterday morning. I need to regroup and fast. "But, uh, how about you crash on the couch?" I suggest. "I'll grab you some pillows and blankets."

I head upstairs and scan Lia's room. There are clothes—tiny things she must have tried and discarded before her date with Arrow—and necklaces and shit on the bed. I pick up the cheap string of beads and set all the clothes on her dresser, sweep the clothes onto the floor, and grab all the blankets and pillows in my arms.

I breathe in the familiar fragrance of her as I head back downstairs.

Tiny is sitting on the couch with his head back against the cushions. His eyes are half closed, so I leave the pillows beside him and set the blankets near his legs.

After I leave the bedding with Tiny, I corral the

dogs up the stairs. I lock them in Lia's room and turn the sound machine and night-light on.

The sun will rise soon, but they know that when their machines are running, they need to be quiet and stay calm.

When he wakes up and I'm gone, I'm only going to give him that much more reason to distrust me.

But it's worth it.

I tiptoe down the stairs and grab the keys to my truck. It'll be a lot quieter than firing up my bike. I need to get out without waking the big man, because if he knew what I have planned... Well, he wouldn't snuggle down on my couch and watch it play out.

I don't leave a note or anything, and as I slip out of my house, I hope it's the last time I ever have to lie to Tiny.

15

LEO

I PULL into the parking lot of my shop and am hit by a ton of emotions.

Rage.

Fear.

Regret.

Sadness.

Everything that I've been working through over the last couple of hours seems to hit me even stronger now, but I do my best to get control of myself.

I unlock the shop and stalk toward my desk. "Asshole," I mutter, thinking about my brother.

I close the folder on the desk and nearly have a heart attack when I notice something moving outside in the parking lot. I get up from the desk and grab an ancient iron wrench.

I head toward the door and grab a wrench because my dumb ass doesn't have a weapon.

When the door is pulled open slowly, I get the shock of my goddamn life. "Tim?" I say, shock and horror at war in my chest.

My brother darts his eyes from left to right, looking like the fox caught in the henhouse. "You alone?" he asks. "Anybody else here?"

"Are you fucking kidding me?" I drop the wrench, and in two long strides, I've got my forearm pressed against Tim's throat. He's not even struggling, not even trying to fight me. "Where the fuck is Lia?"

"Who?" Tim coughs, and it's then I can see it. He's in a bad way. His eyes are rimmed with red, and he's pale.

I shove him once more, hard against the door, but then I release him. "You're drug sick," I seethe. "You're on what? Heroin?" I turn and start to walk away before I realize I need Tim alive, with me, if I want to make a trade for Lia, but I still don't know if he's the one who's got her.

"You disappear for a year and leave me with the

fallout? I oughta fucking call the cops and turn you in right now."

I make like I'm going to pick up my phone, but Tim stops me. "You call, I'm dead," he says simply. But he drops down in the chair opposite my desk and covers his face in his hands. "I'm probably dead anyway. Just—whatever, Leo."

He shocks me by bursting into tears. Actual grown man fucking crying tears. "It's so goddamn good to see you. I thought… I–I thought I'd never see you again. How are you?"

He makes me sick, and the tears make me feel nothing.

"How am I?" I shout. "How am I? How the fuck can you come in here 'little bro'ing' me when you left me? You left, Tim! What the fuck do you think I'm supposed to say, seeing you like this? Do you know what I've been through because of you?"

I pick up the wrench I dropped, and I throw it at the wall of the shop, and it bounces off the cinder block.

"Whoa, stay cool," he urges. "Hear me out."

"Hear you out?" I walk over to the wrench, grab it off the floor, and head back toward Tim with it. "No, you asshole. You hear me out. The woman I love was kidnapped. Because of you. Now I either have to hand you over to the assholes who have her, or I don't know what. They kill her? Worse? And that's only what your bullshit has cost me over the last few hours."

"Aw fuck, brother..." Tim sinks lower in the chair, covering his face with his hands. "Somebody got your girl? Are you sure?"

"I'm fucking sure," I snarl.

I come around to his chair and get in his face. Now, he's nothing to me. He's the reason my life is in the toilet and being sucked down the goddamn drain. He holds my future and Lia's life in his ruined hands.

"Are you behind this?" I demand. I pull out my phone and show him the text. "My girl for you," I grit out. "They want you, so they took her."

Tim looks around the shop wildly. "Do they know anything?" he asks.

"Anything about what?" I demand.

"About me," he says. "Do you think they know how to find me?"

"Think about it, Einstein," I say, using the slam we used on each other when we were kids and did something incredibly stupid. "Would they bother kidnapping a girl if they knew how to get to you?"

Tim gets up out of the chair, but I grab his

shirt, not letting him walk away. I catch a whiff of him, and it's obvious he's been on the run. He smells rank, and I can feel his bones beneath his shirt.

"It's not a good idea for you to leave," I say. "Not until I get my girl home safe."

Tim nods. "I know what they want."

"So, you're not behind this." I need to hear him say it. "You didn't kidnap my girlfriend as a ploy to throw off Arrow?"

"Arrow?" He seems totally confused. "Fuck. Arrow came to you, didn't he?"

"You thought he wouldn't?" I snap. "You put up my goddamn house."

"Our house," Tim corrects quietly.

"It's my goddamn house!" I scream, shaking him by his bony shoulders. "You motherfucking left me and ran off. That's when it stopped being *ours*."

Once I start, I can't stop. I'm screaming in rage.

"Do you know the bank took this place? I almost lost Gramps's shop. The truck. Everything! Because of you! Because of your drugs. Because of your lies. Because you're a selfish prick!"

Tim hangs his head. He doesn't defend himself. Doesn't try to stop any of the accusations flying from my mouth. It's like he's running through the same memories I am. The kids that we were. How we only had each other. How the two of us were alone until Gramps took us in—and even after that.

"We ran a business together for what—how many years?" I ask him. "After we lost Gramps, I thought we'd always have each other's backs. We'd always have each other."

"It's good you found someone," he says quietly. "Someone you can rely on. Someone you can make a future with. You can't do that with me," he says. "I'm wasted, Leo. I'm a waste." He swallows hard and scratches a bunch of tiny scabs growing in the webs of skin between his fingers. "Been addicted a long time," he admits. "Since high school."

"You've been on the run," I say, accusing him.

He nods. "Doping to deal. It's always been my way."

"Doping to deal? With life?"

"Can't help it, man. I've tried to get clean, okay?" Tim stares at his hands. "I thought when I got arrested, that would be the end of the run? I was relieved, to be honest. Happy, almost."

I watch my older brother talk, and I look for signs of the guy I used to worship, look up to. I can see the features of his face—the nose, the color of his eyes—as familiar to me as my own are, but he's like a stranger now.

Distracted.

Fidgety.

Filthy.

It scares me that someone I loved so much could be so different. So completely strange to me that I'm not even sure I can love this person in front of me. Not that he's going to give me the chance.

"So, what changed?" I demand. "Why the fuck did you run off a year ago? You left me with nothing, and they took it, Tim. They took it all. The building is gone, seized by the bank and sold."

He seems incapable of doing anything but nodding and agreeing. "Juliette," he says. "I was gonna tell you about her, but we were both hooked on the shit. Maintenance-level stuff. I knew you'd freak out if you knew I was actively using, let alone had a girlfriend who was also using."

He looks down at the floor.

"I was spending like three grand a week to support us," he says.

"Three grand? Where did you get that kind of money?"

That kind of money going out on bags of smack... No wonder we lost the business.

"I just stopped paying the mortgage on the property, man. The drugs kept going faster and faster. But I love Juliette. She's something special. She's got a degree. She's got potential."

"She's a junkie, just like you."

"Well, yeah, she was," he says. "But do you understand how goddamn hard it is to get clean in this country? How much the detox programs are?"

I shrug, not in the mood for a lecture about fairness and access to health care from a guy who shot an entire family legacy into his veins.

"Don't you think if we had options that didn't include ruining my kid brother's life, we would have taken them?" Tim's getting worked up now too, but it's weak. I can see he's defeated. He's hoping I can see things through his eyes.

"I can't imagine," I say. I can't help laying on the sarcasm. "Because while I got up every goddamn morning and worried how many more days I'd have before the bank took our business, you were out there high as a kite, living your junkie dream."

Tim nods a slow, painful nod. "If this is a dream, man...you don't want to live the nightmare."

"Promise me you didn't take her?" I press. "You

have nothing to do with my girlfriend's disappearance?"

Tim shakes his head. "Fuck no. You know me better than that, man."

"I used to know you." I wave my hand between us. "The person in front of me, I don't know what he's capable of, and at this point, I don't care to know.

"Who are these assholes who want you enough to kidnap and hold somebody for ransom?"

Tim shudders. "Bad dudes."

That was the wrong thing to say. I get up from my seat and round the desk, but Tim stops me before I can start swinging.

"I know what they want, Leo."

"So do I," I say, grabbing my phone. "They want you. And I'm going to hand you over to them right now."

"Wait. Leo, please." His hands shake as he tries to stand, and he collapses back against the chair in defeat.

But there is something in his voice that makes me stop. Makes me set down that phone before I send the text that ends this. "I'm listening," I grit out. "You have ten seconds to change my mind."

"I know who has her, and I know what they

want." He looks me square in the eyes. I want to believe he's telling the truth.

"How can I trust you, Tim? How can I be so sure? You gonna just take me to them? Send over a text message and be, like, sorry, guys, small mix-up? Take me and not my brother's girlfriend?"

Tim looks at me and raises his brows. "Can I get up?" he asks.

"You planning on running?" I ask.

He shakes his head.

"I'll fucking tackle you and break your face if you do. The kidnappers just need to be able to identify you. I can do a lot of damage and still leave your face, looking like you."

Tim gets up from the chair and motions for me to follow him. He pulls a key ring from the pocket of his jeans and throws it to me.

"What the fuck is this?" I ask. There is a single key on a cheap plastic key ring. I recognize it instantly. "How did you…"

He shrugs. "Always kept it with me. No matter what."

I finger the plastic like it's as fragile as a memory. Because it is. The diamond-shaped plastic is red and has a chip in it. On one side in barely readable ink is the logo and address of a motel.

"The Red Pelican." As I say the words, all the years collapse into this one moment.

Tim nods. "Any time I've ever had anything that mattered, I lock it up and use this keyring to protect the key." He sighs and scrubs a hand across his face. Tears still wet his cheeks, but he's not actively crying. It's like the tears are flowing in spite of himself. "All these years, no matter where I was or what fucked-up state I was in, I never lost it. No matter how fucked up I got, as long as I held on to this, I knew I could come back."

My parents stayed at the Red Pelican on their honeymoon—which was basically a one-night stay in the cheap motel away from the prying eyes of two sets of disapproving parents. It was all they could afford, one night away from their after-school jobs when my mom got pregnant in high school and her parents kicked her out.

My gramps and gram took both kids in for a few months, until Tim was born and they were back on their feet. Mom and Dad spent a weekend at the Red Pelican every single year for their anniversary after that. Mom bought the key chain for a dollar to remember their honeymoon by.

She used that key chain every day for as long as I knew her, as long as I can remember. House keys, car keys. No matter what hook it was hung on, what purse it was buried at the bottom of, that diamond-shaped plastic key chain from the Red Pelican is part of the fabric of the memories I have of my parents. Of our family. It's where our family started.

That key chain was the one thing after they passed away that was recovered from the accident that took them away from us.

"Why?" I demand. "Why give this to me now? What the fuck do you want me to do with it, Tim? Forgive you because you kept a memento of our parents while you were shooting thousands of dollars of shit into your arms? That because you saved the key chain, I shouldn't care that you lost our fucking business?" I shake my head at him, wanting him to feel even worse about all this than he's making me feel.

I can't fucking save him. I can't stop him from wanting drugs, doing drugs. I sure as hell couldn't stop him from selling drugs even though we had a house, a business. I thought we were doing all right, us two. On our own. But he didn't love me enough to stay clean. He didn't care enough about his little brother to not take it all away to feed his own pain.

Tim lowers his eyes, his chin practically touching his bony chest. "You can make me feel as bad as you want to, and I promise you, it won't be half as bad as I feel about myself on my best day. Give it all you've got, Leo. I'm a worthless piece of shit, and I let you down. I know that. And I can't say enough I'm sorrys to make it okay. But I told you. I know who has your girlfriend, and I know what they want."

"Yeah, asshole," I seethe. "They want you."

Tim cocks his head. "Well, that's what they said. They think they want me because they think I have all the shit I stole from them."

My heart sinks. Of course, he did.

Arrow was right.

I'm not the only one my brother double-crossed.

"What do you have, Tim? What did you do?"

He walks up to me and points to the rusted-out piece-of-shit car that's been sitting in my shop for days. "Open it. Trunk."

My mouth drops open in disbelief. "You?" I ask, dumbfounded. "This goddamn Cadillac is yours?"

Tim nods. "That engine is fucked, right? I wondered if you'd suspect it was some kind of message from me. Remember what Gramps used to say? You think hiring a pro is expensive—"

"Try hiring an amateur." I finish the phrase that

I must have heard hundreds, maybe thousands of times growing up.

I can't believe it. "So that woman, the one who had this towed in…"

"That's Juliette. My wife." He looks sad. But then he firms his lips. "I know what my girl means to me. Let me do what I can to help get yours back."

I take the Red Pelican key chain and pop the trunk of the Cadillac and take a look inside.

"Hoooooolllly fuck."

16

LEO

"TIM...WHAT THE FUCK." I can't even believe what I'm looking at. "What is..." The questions are flying out of my mouth faster than I can think to form them.

Tim nods. "I know," he says. "I know. It's a lot of money."

"What the... Are you out of your fucking mind?" My stomach sinks, and my palms start to sweat. "Where did you get this money?" This is serious money. Stolen, I assume, from some seriously bad people. "Is this drug money?"

I start to panic.

Maybe it would have been better if I'd found a body in the trunk. This? This is the big time.

The risk he exposed me to by keeping this here…it's even worse than him actively making me lose the business or the house. He's made me an unwitting accomplice to crimes I can't even comprehend have taken place.

"What the fuck did you do this for?" I'm pacing now, terrified. "What if someone found out it was here? Who did you steal this from? What were you going to do with this?"

I know before he admits it that he was *not* going to use this money to save my house. A selfish, drug-abusing user would rather steal money from bad guys and steal the house right out from under me than face the music the honest way. Not to mention his total disregard for the danger stashing this shit in my shop brought down on me, my business.

"You're going back to fucking prison," I say, grabbing my phone.

In the heat of the moment, I consider it. I consider dialing 9-1-1 and letting the cops pick up my deadbeat brother and take his ass away for good, but Tim's hand on my arm stops me.

"This is the only thing keeping Lia alive," he reminds me. "That money is what they want. They only want me because they think I have it."

And just like that, I hang up the phone.

"So, now what?" I ask. "I'm guessing you're not going to show up with me at midnight and let me hand you over to the assholes who have Lia. That or show up with a bag of cash and propose a new deal."

Tim shakes his head. "You don't have to. I have a plan."

"I already don't like it," I mutter, but he's my best chance to get Lia back.

"Give me a break, Leo." Tim is pleading with me. He's not being shitty.

He looks scared.

"I can't go to prison. Locked up away from Juliette. Away from life. I can't. I won't do it."

"You're a fucking drug dealer, Tim. You deserve it."

"I'm an addict, Leo. If I could get clean, do you really think I'd deal? I hate this shit. Okay? I hate it! I hate how it makes me feel, how it makes me think. I hate being a junkie. And don't even pretend that's not what I am. I know what you think of me. I'm not trying to pretend I'm a hero. But bank robbers get out of jail with less time than they'll give me if I go back."

"So, what?" I demand. "You were going to let me lose the house while you and Juliette and this nice wad of cash sailed off into the sunset? Until what? You shoot that money up your veins, and then you're broke, high, and back in the goddamn clink?"

He walks up to me and looks me right in the eye. "No, Leo. Okay? That was never the plan. There's a place in Costa Rica..." He gets this dreamy look in his eyes. "Juliette and I planned on going down there and getting clean. We could pay ten thousand for both of us, spend a few months in rehab down there, and have enough money left over to start new lives."

I don't know shit about Costa Rica, but that sounds like a pipe dream to me. "Well, as happy as I want to be that you had this whole happy ending planned out for you and your wife, your entire plan still hinged on screwing me out of the business, the house...fucking me, Tim. Your plan all along has been to fuck me."

"You see that bag?" He points to a small grocery store sack.

"Uh, yeah?" It's empty and sitting beside the canvas bags that are piled high with cash.

"Juliette was going to leave that for you. Filled with cash." He grimaces at me. "It probably wouldn't have been enough to save the house," he admits. "But I told her to leave you at least fifty. It would have been something. It would have made a dent."

"A dent," I echo. "A dent is all you have room for when it comes to your brother."

I slam the trunk of the Cadillac closed and turn on him. "Now what, Tim? You're wasting my time. I don't give a fuck about your future and your bullshit lies about getting clean and starting over. Some thugs have Lia, and they want you. You have their cash, which you want to run off with to Costa Rica. I don't see a happy ending to this story."

Tim huffs a huge sigh. I look closely at him. I still can't believe this guy is my blood. My brother. He looks nothing like the healthy, fit guy who used to play beach volleyball with his friends.

"I can take you to where they're keeping Lia."

"What?" I bolt upright. "Why the fuck didn't you lead with that? You know where she is? How do you know?"

"Barry Kasterson," he says. "Barry's one of the suppliers I used to work for."

He explains how he got out on bail, reaching out to Josh, his high school buddy, for help with the bond. But I stop him right there because I know this part of the story. I didn't know that he planned on fucking over Arrow too.

Intentionally.

"Wait, wait, wait." I'm seething, seeing red, and I don't even give a shit about Arrow. "You're telling me you went to a high school buddy for your bond when you knew full well you were going to skip out?" I ask.

The layers of how my brother planned to fuck people are just...I can't believe it.

"No. Jesus, Leo. Would you give it a rest? I get that you think I'm a total asshole." He calms down and sits. "I was planning on fighting the charges. There were problems with my arrest and some evidence shit, I don't know. I had a lawyer for a while. I got out on bail, tried to get a real job. Tried for months, actually. I was gonna get clean and fight the charges, Leo. I was."

He looks at me, and all I see is the ruin.

The futility.

"I couldn't go straight, Leo. Nobody wants to hire a white trash motherfu..."

"Shut the fuck up already. Take me to Lia, or I'm going to end you right here."

He wipes his face with the back of a sleeve. "We give that to Barry, we take Lia, and we're even."

"You think it's that easy?" I ask. "We take their hostage, leave the cash, and what? You got a greeting card? Maybe we should stop at the market for a thank-you note. Make sure they know who left the bag of fucking cash in place of their prisoner."

"It's the best shot we have."

"No," I correct him. "It's the best shot you have. I can call the cops right now and have you, and this Barry motherfucker, put away for a long, long time."

Tim is quiet. "What about this?" he asks. "I'll go with you to get Lia. If she's safe, I'll hand Barry the money myself."

I think about that for a second. "You mean we go together? You'd bring me to the drug dealer you stole from, return his money, and help me save my girl?"

Tim nods. "Barry's an asshole, but he's small time. He's no murderer. Why do you think I stole from him? He's small enough that he trusted an asshole out on bail to deal for him. I really think this could work. He wants his money, Leo. He only wants what's his."

I want what's mine too.

Lia.

She's the only thing that matters.

Not the house.

Not my brother.

Not even the memories.

I think it over. It sounds like an absolutely terrible plan. "All right," I tell him. I hold out my hand. "Until this is all done, I'm going to need the key for that Caddy, and when it's over, you're not forgiven. You're not in my life." I motion for Tim to sit. "This asshole isn't expecting to make the trade until midnight tonight," I tell him. "I need to make a call first."

I punch in a number.

Forty-five minutes later, Dog pulls up to the shop in his truck with a flatbed trailer on the back.

I head out front to meet him.

"What's the news, Prospect?" He jumps down out of the truck and checks his watch. "Ain't it a little early for auto repair work? Tiny would have a shit to end all shits if he knew you were working when his kid is…"

But just then, my brother walks out of the shop, his head hung low.

"Dog," I say cautiously. "This is my brother. Tim."

DOG EYES me with a look that can only be described as "Boy, have you lost your mind?"

I press the Red Pelican key chain into his hand. "Don't lose this," I tell him. "Tow it home."

"My home," he says, confirming that I mean the compound, not my house.

"Yep." I nod.

Dog is looking really uncomfortable.

"Tim," I say. "We can head out now that Dog's here. You wanna grab your shit?"

Tim nods and heads back into the shop to grab the sack of money. As soon as we're alone, I give Dog the bare minimum.

"Give this key to Josh," I tell him. I press the Red Pelican key chain into his fist.

"Any instructions?" he asks. "Anything you want me to say to Tiny?"

I shake my head. Tim's already coming back

through the door, cradling the cash behind him so Dog can't see it.

"Nope," I tell him loudly, acting like everything's all good. "My brother and I are going to handle things from here. I'll be back soon with Lia."

"Should I—" Dog is standing there looking confused and highly concerned.

I shake my head. I don't want Tim to suspect I've asked Dog to alert Arrow.

"We'll be back," I tell Dog and motion for Tim to get into my truck.

There are no cars parked in the lot, so I'm wondering how Tim even got here. I wait until Dog has the Caddy on the flatbed before I lock the shop and watch him pull away with Tim's toxic haul. All that money. I seriously can't believe it. I say a small prayer that nothing happens to Dog on the way. The last thing I need is this getting any messier than it is.

"You're no dumbass," Tim says, watching as his entire life is towed away.

"Just insurance," I say. "How'd you get here if you didn't drive?"

"Juliette dropped me off," he says. "She was supposed to wait ten minutes, and if I didn't come out, to go wait for me at your house."

"My house?" I start at that. "Tiny's at my house, Tim. If she goes there and Tiny..."

"Who the fuck is Tiny?" he asks.

"Lia's dad. I called him when she went missing." I look at him sideways as I back my truck out of the lot. "Wait a fucking minute. Did you know that Lia was taken? Did you show up here to make things right because you knew my girlfriend had been kidnapped?"

Tim fiddles with the handle on the plastic bag of cash.

"Hide that shit, you idiot," I snap at him. "We get pulled over and I got a wanted felon carrying a bag of cash? Jesus."

"What the hell do you expect me to do with this?" Tim snaps, and slides the cash under the passenger seat and leans back. "I'm sorry, man."

"For what now?" I ask.

"Boat's leaving tonight. I'm leaving. Juliette and I are going to hop a boat. Sail to Costa Rica tonight."

"You were gonna break in to the building and steal the money back?"

Tim is silent.

"We have security cameras, you dumb fuck," I say.

"Juliette scoped them out. That's why we brought the car in to you. We needed a safe place to store the cash until we could get a boat squared away that could take us all the way. You took like fifteen minutes looking at the car to tell her how long you'd need it. More than enough time for her to assess the system. She knew right away all you had were those cheap internet motion-sensor cams."

I huff a series of curses under my breath. I was better off when my brother was on the run, far the fuck away from me. If Lia hadn't gotten dragged into this, he'd be on a boat tonight, and I'd be none the wiser. Although, I'd probably have been stuck with a useless Cadillac and a lot of unanswered questions.

"I'm sorry, Leo." Tim looks at the radio before reaching across the dash to flip it on.

I slap his hand away. "Fuck you," I snarl. "I need an address."

He tells me the address, and I punch it into my phone's GPS.

"What are you doing?" Tim asks, suddenly paranoid.

I hold the screen of my phone up to him to show him the navigation. "You wanna tell me where to turn, or should I use the app?" I can't keep the shittiness out of my voice. It would serve him right if I called the police, fire department, the local news, and God himself.

He reaches for the radio again. Again, I slap his hand away.

I don't wait for him to respond. This isn't a road trip. Passenger doesn't control the music.

"You're an asshole, Tim."

17

LIA

I HEAR SOMETHING.

Mikey hears it too. He lifts his head and listens, a light whimper breaking past his toothless lips.

I scoot a few inches away from Mikey. He doesn't seem to get that he'd be better off not snuggling up to me.

"Mikey," I urge on a harsh whisper. "Go to your corner. Go."

I'm afraid to talk too loud and attract the attention of the cameras, but I'd feel worse if those horrible people came back and Mikey got punished for wanting a little human affection. A little love. He retreats into his corner and huddles in the dark, and my heart breaks. The closer I get to freedom, the less afraid I am.

They haven't hurt me, and I must be pretty far in the middle of nowhere if they left me here for any amount of time. Even with the threat of Mikey —who, let's be real, isn't much of a threat—how bad must they be, really?

But I remember they want to trade me for another person. Tim—Leo's brother. A drug addict and dealer. So, who the hell knows what these people are or want?

All I know is I hear footsteps outside the building, and Mikey is starting to whine.

"Shh." I urge him to be quiet.

No matter who it is, a stranger or my kidnappers, it can't hurt for him to keep it down.

I lie still as a stone and close my eyes as the door opens.

"What the fuck's going on in there? Did you not listen to what I said?"

I sit up as fast as I can, but it's hard with my wrists tied. "It's not me!" I cry out. "There are people outside making him crazy. You have to know I'm not doing anything."

"You stupid bitch." The guy grabs my arm and yanks me up to standing.

I don't even think he notices Mikey, but if he does, he doesn't care.

"Ouch!" I know he doesn't care about this either, but he's hurting me. "Stop it!" I shout. "I didn't do anything."

"I wouldn't say things are fine… Someone set off the cameras."

"It wasn't me," I say quickly, trying to get free from his grip. "I swear, it wasn't me."

The door swings open, and I flinch as B whirls around, tightening his grip on me.

"Leo!" I scream from excitement and fear. Tears are streaming down my face.

Leo looks me over, and I can tell he wants to run to me. His fists are balled up at his sides, and he's glaring. He sees the bucket beside me. My hands in restraints.

B gives Leo a wicked glare. He pulls a gun from the back of his pants and points it at Leo.

I gasp as my knees buckle, but B only tightens his hold on me, no doubt bruising my skin.

"I don't think you want to shoot me, *Barry*," Leo says, using what I assume is the guy's first name. "Considering I came to make that trade we agreed on."

Barry lowers his gun away from Leo's head. "I'm a reasonable enough man if you've got your brother nearby."

"I'd like to make sure my girl is okay before we complete our business."

"Some girl she is," Barry sneers. "She was out with that bounty hunter asshole when we picked her up. I'm happy to give her back, but…" He looks back at me with an expression that's pure evil. "She looks like an ungrateful whore from where I sit."

"Leo," I say, "there's another one. A woman."

Barry stops my warning with a swift slap across the face.

I'm stunned and drop to the concrete floor, bruising my knees.

"You motherfucker," Leo hisses. "You really don't want your money, do you?"

That gets Barry's attention. "What money? What are you talking about? We were swapping your girl for your brother."

Leo holds up one hand and pretends to count out loud. "Fifty, seventy… No, I'm pretty damn sure it was seventy-five grand my brother stole from you. That's what you want back from him? Isn't it? You want the money? Or did you just want to keep my brother tied up here in your little love shack while I keep whatever it is that Tim stole from you?"

Barry snarls. "Stop fucking around. You want what's yours, you give me what's mine."

"Well, you have to choose, Barry." Leo rocks back on his heels. "You want your stolen drug money, or you want the junkie who stole it from you?" He motions toward the door. "Cuz I found both. I can keep the money and give you Tim, or…"

"Give me the goddamn money!" Barry shouts, and in that second, the doors of the warehouse fly open.

A half-dozen police officers and DEA agents swarm the warehouse. Before I know what's happening, Barry is on his knees and in cuffs.

Another officer has his female accomplice, the skanky bitch from Checkers, in cuffs too. I don't know where she came from, but right now, I don't care.

They got him.

They got her.

Leo rushes over and grabs me, pulling me close, but we don't fit together with my hands still bound.

"I need something," Leo shouts.

An officer comes up to me and cuts the ties from my wrists. Paramedics have arrived too, and they are wheeling in a gurney for me.

"I'm fine," I promise, crawling into Leo's arms and clinging to him, crying. "Leo, Leo."

"Baby," he says as he pulls his head back from mine and holds my face in his hands.

"And they drugged me, and I got sick. I have to smell horrible."

"I don't give a shit," Leo says. He claims my mouth in a ravenous kiss, and I can't resist him. His touch melts me, and I open my mouth, tears flooding my face and his.

He presses his forehead to mine. "I love you," I whisper. "Leo, I always have. All that bullshit about being friends, just being roommates—"

"Stop." He tilts my chin so I'm looking into his eyes. "Lia, I've loved you since that first day you and your girl crew came into town in your crazy van with all your glitter and green juices. And I will love you forever. No more roommates, no more playing house. I want you to be mine. Forever."

We cling to each other, kissing until the para-medics interrupt to check me out. I sit on the stretcher and answer a few questions about what happened, what I've been through. They look over my wrists, and when they hear I was drugged, they insist on taking me to the hospital for a checkup.

"Fine," I say, "but my boyfriend has to come or I'm not going."

Leo stands beside the gurney, holding my hands

261

between both of his. He's not saying anything, but tears are streaming down his cheeks.

"Lia!" a voice barks from the far side of the warehouse.

"Dad." I jump from the stretcher, squealing at the sight of Tiny. My knees wobble when I start to run, the pain from the bruising surprising me, but it doesn't slow me down. Not by much.

I wrap my arms as far as I can around my dad, squeezing my eyes shut. "How did you get here?" I ask. "How did you know what was going on?"

"We'll have plenty of time for explanations," he says, releasing me.

He glares at Leo, and I know that because I'm out of harm's way doesn't mean that anything is forgiven. I feel terrible that Leo's days in the MC might be over.

Again, because of me.

"You found your brother?" I ask. "Is he okay? What's going to happen with the house? What about all the stuff you said to Barry? About the money—was that true?"

While the police take pictures and haul Barry away, Leo explains what went down.

"No," I gasp, totally stunned. "Was that little

lady who brought in the car Juliette? She was there all the time?"

Leo nods. "That's why I couldn't reach the client after she dropped off the car. Burner phone. She'd checked out our shitty security cameras and figured they could pretty easily break in to the shop and get the cash when they were ready to go on the run. We met her before we ever knew she was connected to my brother, and by then... I didn't remember her face at all. I was too focused on her fucked-up engine to remember her face."

"So, they were going to go on the run," I say. The reality of that makes me really sad. And I know it must gut Leo. That fucking sucks.

Tim was going to leave his brother high and dry. He would totally have lost his house. "How did you find him? How'd you stop him?"

Leo explains that he'd gone into the shop while Tiny crashed at our place. Tim showed up, and they came up with a plan to swap the cash Tim had stolen for me.

"But the police?" I think I'm lost.

Leo grinned. "I had Dog come by and tow away the Cadillac with the rest of Tim's cash in it. I figured it was insurance either way. Juliette wouldn't know where it was and couldn't steal it and run off.

And if things went well here, the money and the car would be safe until Tim and I got back with you."

"What if things didn't go well? What if they wanted to kill your brother or something?"

"That's why they called me." Josh stood back from the fray, but I motion him forward so he can fill me in.

"Lia…" he starts. "I don't even know what to say."

I step forward and wrap my arms around him. "I'm sorry, Josh," I say. "It was a stupid idea. I should have listened to my heart and found another way to help Leo. I put myself in harm's way, and you, too. And I wasn't exactly playing fair. It was never really a love triangle. I love Leo," I say. "Am in love with Leo."

"Oh, goddamn it." Tiny sighs and storms away, muttering under his breath. "I goddamn knew it!"

I giggle even though Leo doesn't look too amused. "He'll get used to it," I remind him.

"I'm not so sure," Leo mutters.

"So, anyway," Josh says, "Leo told Dog to call me, let me know about the money and the drugs."

"Drugs?" I don't remember that part.

Leo nods. "Yeah, turns out my brother didn't

only have cash in the trunk. He had a little travel insurance in the glove box."

"Miss?" the paramedic interrupts. "We really need to go."

I start toward the ambulance, my hand locked with Leo's, when I see an officer taking Mikey away.

"I want him," I tell the officer. "His name is Mikey. I want him."

"I'm going to have to take him down to animal control," the cop says. "If he's cleared to adopt, you can take it up with—"

"I want him," I insist and look to my father. "Dad, make it happen."

Tiny lifts his brows at the officer. "Which animal control location you headed to?" He looks at me. "Cool your jets, kid. I'll handle it."

I climb into the ambulance, and the paramedics start checking all my vitals. They give me a little juice plus something to calm me down.

At the hospital, they draw blood, ask me a million questions, and examine me, and Leo stays by my side through the whole entire thing.

I'm exhausted, and I want to get home to my dogs.

"Relax," Leo assures me, rubbing my arm. "Tiny's at the house. I gave him instructions. He'll feed the girls and let them out. He promised me he'll stay until we're home."

The doctor comes into the room to check me, but all I want is to know when I can go home.

After sleeping on a concrete floor, I want to feel my own bed, my own sheets against my skin. And I want to hold Leo. I want nothing more than that, an endless horizon of days holding him so tight against me that I'll never let him go.

"Hello, Miss Dove."

"Can I go?" I ask, growing impatient.

"We did find something in your tests. I don't think it's cause for concern right now, but we'd like to keep you overnight."

Leo's immediately on edge. "What is it?" he demands. "I thought you said they didn't hurt her?"

"We don't think they did," the doctor reassures us. "But because we don't know what they used to drug you, we'd like to make sure."

"But I'm fine now," I say. I really don't want to stay here another minute longer than I have to. "Can't I follow up with my primary doctor if anything seems off?"

The doctor nods. "Of course, yes, but we think it's best for the baby if you stay overnight to make sure he or she is okay."

"Wait…" My mouth drops open, or at least I think it does. I'm looking at Leo, and I feel like we're mirroring each other's expressions. "What?"

"The other night on the couch," Leo says, his eyes wide. "When I had the whiskey…"

I shake my head and start laughing. "Babe, that was like, what, two nights ago? You don't get pregnant that fast."

"If you'll let us, we'd like to keep you overnight and get that ultrasound scheduled first thing. If things look good, you can go home after that." She looks from me to Leo. "I'm sorry you had to find out this way, but…congratulations, Mom and Dad."

As soon as she leaves, Leo drops down into the chair beside the bed. He looks pale. "A dad? I'm going to be a shit dad. I thought we were careful."

"Babe," I say gently, reaching for his hand. "Come back up here."

He climbs onto the hospital bed beside me, and we interlace our fingers.

"How many times have we been pretty wasted when we fucked?"

Leo shrugs. "I don't know. I mean… A lot?"

"How many of those times do you think maybe we forgot to grab a condom or were too swept up in the moment to really care?"

Leo shrugs again. "I guess… A lot."

"And don't say such things about yourself. You're going to be an amazing daddy. You poor thing," I say, squeezing his hand and resting my head back against the bed.

"What?" Leo asks. "Why?"

I give him a snarky grin. "My daddy's going to murder you dead."

THE DOOR to my hospital room opens, and my dad's head fills the opening. "You up?" he asks, looking me straight in the eyes.

"Do I look up?" I tease him and place my finger against my lips before ticking my head toward a sleeping Leo. He hasn't left my side all night.

"Kid looks like shit," Dad mutters, coming next to the bed and grabbing my hand. "I was so worried, baby. So damn worried."

"We're okay, Daddy. I knew one of you would find me, and we'd get out of this okay," I sort of lie. I had faith in them, but whether or not we'd be okay…who the fuck knew.

"We?" Dad asks, his eyebrows pulling down in

the center, causing his forehead to crease more than normal.

"Don't freak out," I whisper.

My words make his eyes widen suddenly. "Who did what to you? I'll kill 'em."

"Daddy," I bite out. "You will not." I move my hand to my stomach. "I'm pregnant."

My father staggers backward, his hand on his chest like I punched him. "You're what? How?"

I stare at him. "You understand how babies are made, Dad."

He shakes his head, trying to regain his composure. "Who?"

My eyes drift to Leo, and my father's head turns to the side, following my gaze. I don't even have a chance to speak before my dad is holding a fistful of Leo's T-shirt in his hand, ripping him out of the chair.

"I should fucking kill you," Dad says as Leo's eyes open wider, and he goes to swing but misses.

"Daddy," I snap. "Stop it."

"You touched my little girl?"

"I... Um..."

"Dad," I plead. "This isn't good for the baby."

My dad's shoulders slump forward, but he doesn't let go of Leo. "Fuck me," he whispers. "I knew you two were fucking around. Knew it in my bones. I thought you two were smarter than this." He shakes his head. "You're nothing but babies yourself, and I'm not old enough to be a gran—" He stops, swallowing hard at the word.

"Grandpa," I say for him. "Surprise, you're going to be a grandpa."

"Like fuck I am."

I giggle. "You are."

"I'm going to be Tiny to everyone, even the kid."

I raise an eyebrow. "Our baby is not calling you Tiny. Don't be ridiculous. You can be Grandpa, Pa, Pawpaw, Gramps, Grandpappy, Granddad…"

"Stop," Dad begs, releasing Leo. "I can't. This is too much."

"Daddy," I whisper and hold out my hand to him.

He takes my fingers in his as he moves back to my bedside, leaving Leo unharmed. "I thought I'd never see you again, baby. I thought about all the years I wasted and fucked away."

"I'm fine. We're fine," I reassure him. "We have the rest of our lives, and you can make up all the missed time you didn't get with me with your grandchild."

He's green, but he doesn't argue.

"You're going to make an awesome grandpa."

"Big Paw."

"What?"

"They can call me Big Paw."

Leo rolls his eyes behind my dad, and I stifle a laugh. "Whatever you want as long as you promise to love the baby more than you love me."

"Impossible," Dad says as he leans over and places a kiss on my forehead.

I'm smiling like an idiot when he turns his face toward Leo. "We're not done dealing with this between us. Man-to-man. Brother-to-brother."

Leo nods, standing tall, but he remains silent.

"Get some rest," Dad says to me. "I'll swing by to see you when you get home."

"Thanks, Daddy."

"Love you, baby."

"Love you too," I tell him, and I mean every word of it.

For as lonely as my childhood was, my adult years have been kicking ass, and I can only see more love in the future.

18

LEO

"LIA? BABY, ARE YOU AWAKE?"

I hear Leo's voice calling to me in my dreams. I squint and bury my face deeper in the pillow. If this is a dream, I want to go right back to sleep.

"Lia?"

The familiar squeak of my bedroom door opening lets me know the voice is real.

"Leo, it's so...*early*..." I moan. "Why are you out of bed? You promised me you'd stay here all week long!"

I've only been home from the hospital for a day. Leo has been a wreck ever since we got home. He's been on the phone constantly, calling Josh for information about Tim. Calling Tiny to check in on the MC. Calling Morris for moral support.

"Babe, it's not early," he tells me. He climbs back into bed beside me, wearing only pajama pants. His chest is bare, as are his feet. "I let the dogs out and fed them. Now I'm back."

He slides under the covers and curls up behind me.

"We should maybe pick a room and share it. Like real couples," I say.

"You're saying we're a real couple now?" He's got his mouth against my hair, and his breath tickles my ear. My body zings to life, and he hasn't even touched me.

"Well, yeah," I say. "We said the words, and we're having a baby together." I roll over to face him.

"Sweet Jesus, Lia," he says, rubbing his forehead. But this time, he doesn't tear his eyes away from me.

I curl my lips into a sleepy grin. "You know I sleep naked, bud. You're getting the full show."

I push the sheets away to give him a view of tits. I prop myself up on an elbow and face him. "Are you really okay?" I ask him.

"My parents were teenage parents," he shares.

"Yeah?" I ask.

He nods. "Tim was an oops."

"We won't have a Tim, Leo," I reassure him. "But if we do, if our kids have problems with addiction or depression, or hate the color pink—which to me, would be absolute agony—we'll love them through it. We'll give them the stable upbringing you and Tim didn't have. We don't have to repeat anyone else's mistakes. We'll make our own, but we can learn from others and do better."

Leo is quiet.

"Whatcha thinking?" I ask.

"I want to do better," he says. "What do you think about us buying our own house? Something new, fresh. Just ours. Something we pick out only for us."

"You going into the club today?" I ask, changing the subject because I think he's overreacting, and this place is home.

"I don't know," he says. "Might. I'll check with Morris later. See what he says."

"If you don't have to go and clean toilets…" I look down at my chest as I reach beneath the sheet to touch myself. I cup my breast in one hand and lift it so if I stretch my tongue out, I can barely reach to lick my erect nipple.

"Jesus, woman." Leo's breaths come in hard puffs. "The things you do to me."

"I have a whole long list of things I'd like you to do to me," I purr. "Some of them require your fingers, some your mouth."

"On your stomach," he demands.

"Oh!" I squeal in delight as he flips me onto my stomach. I turn my face so I can breathe and jam a pillow under my stomach.

Leo moves my legs apart and settles his face above my ass. "God, your body, babe. I fucking love it."

He slides two fingers into his mouth, which I can tell he's done when he strokes me. He palms my ass with his other hand and kneads my cheeks, spreading them wide so he can look at my pussy.

I don't know why I love being exposed to him this way, every part of me vulnerable and laid bare.

I close my eyes and let him work his magic on my ass cheeks, kneading and massaging them until I'm trembling with need. He gets to work with his mouth. He sinks between my legs, and I feel the sweet, soft strokes of his tongue against my clit. He works it lightly and then harder, sucking and stroking until I am pressing my ass in the air like a hussy, greedy and wanting more.

I flip onto my back and spread my legs wide. "I want you here," I demand, pointing to my tits.

"And here," I say, tapping my finger against my lips.

"Any particular order?" he asks with a grin.

I lift my breast in my hand, and Leo obliges. He sucks me into his mouth, and I see stars.

I close my eyes, and for a moment, I see the cold, dark concrete floor where I rested my head. I hear the angry voice of Barry, that fuckwad, and his cold-ass skanky girlfriend.

I take a deep breath and remind myself where I am.

I'm home. I'm safe. Leo is with me. They can't get me. They never wanted me. I'm safe.

"Baby?" Leo releases my breast and meets my eyes. "Where'd you go?"

"Back there," I admit. "But just for a minute. I'm okay."

He climbs beside me and tugs the covers up to our shoulders. "Barry is in jail, and he's not going to get out for a very long time. And that woman, Gretchen, she's an accomplice, but she's gone too. Women's prison upstate, probably. They won't hurt you again, Lia. I won't ever let anyone hurt you ever again."

"I know," I say. And I mean it. "I'm okay. I

know you're here, and they're there. It's just… My brain's going to need some time."

He nods. "Tell me what you need, baby, and I'll do it."

His face looks so earnest. He's so concerned. But more than just concern for me and my mental health, I see what I've wanted to see on Leo's face for so, so long.

I don't think I ever realized how badly I needed it. He loves me. I know he's said it, but there's something about seeing that love written all over someone's face that makes it feel even more real than a house. Even more real than the words. Even more real than the babies we're going to bring into the world together.

"Just love me," I say. "Exactly the way you are."

"How exactly?" he asks, reaching between my legs under the blankets. "Are we talking love you like this?"

He strokes me gently, working his fingers lightly down my thighs, searing my skin with firm movements, kneading, and waking up every fiber of my legs.

His steady rhythm quickens my pulse. The closer his fingers get to my core, the needier I become. I feel like I'm melting inside, my pussy clenching as molten heat floods my core.

"That…That's what I mean," I croak, wriggling and working my body against his touch.

He bends his head to reach my breast and goes back to work on my nipples. He isn't teasing the tender skin this time, but he's nibbling and nipping, working his teeth against my erect tips. I gasp and clench the sheet in my hands, but he's not going to slow up on this seductive tease. He alternates his love bites with puffs of hot air, then cool, tingling breaths against my inflamed skin.

I release my death grip on the sheets and work my fingers through his beautiful, thick hair. I arch my back to bring more of myself into his mouth, and he pulls a hand away from my pussy to knead my breast while he sucks it.

The sounds I'm making are greedy and loud. I won't hold back now. He's my man, and I'm his woman, and I want every touch, every breath to be rewarded with unrestrained me. "Fuck, baby, yes… I love you so much!"

I open my eyes to see if my words spook him, but they have the opposite effect. Leo's eyes go black. He jams my tit into his mouth and flicks his tongue, working every inch of my nipple until I'm a throbbing, writhing mess.

"Baby, please." I tap my fingers against my mouth. "Get over here."

Leo slides out from beneath the blankets and kneels over my face. I look up at his gorgeous body. His thighs frame my face. I reach up and claw my nails down the sides of his legs, and he throws his head back and groans.

I slip a hand between his legs and cup his balls.

"Lia," he gasps, sucking in air.

"Lower," I demand.

When he sinks closer to my face, I lift my chin and flick my tongue gently along the seam of his sac. It drives him insane, and I grip his dick in my hands, gently stroking in time with my licks.

"Lia... You're gonna..."

"I'm not going to stop is what I'm going to do," I purr against his tender skin. I adjust my neck and motion with my fingers for him to lie on his back beside me. "Too much work this way," I laugh.

I straddle his lap and, without any warning, plunge my mouth onto his erection. I stick my booty in the air and suck him in, swirling my tongue on the underside of the tip before plunging him as deep as I can take him.

He's completely lost in the pleasure I'm giving him. His body trembles slightly. His eyes are closed, and he gently weaves his hands through the waves of my hair.

"You good?" I ask, lifting my face from his cock.

"Ah, um, I…" he mumbles incoherently, an adorable grin on his face.

"Leo, I love you."

"I love you, babe. Now, please, would you fuck me already?" he begs.

I slide down onto him, and we both suck in air at the sensation that overcomes us both. I'm launched into another dimension when Leo is inside me. I work my hips back and forth, barely rocking so his cock shifts slightly inside me. I like to work him as long as I can, and this gentle start means I'm going to explode hard and fast when I get there.

I settle him deep inside, rolling my hips. My eyes are closed, and I reach down to lace my fingers with his. I use the leverage to lift myself up slightly and bounce on his cock.

"Goddamn," he cries, and I groan at the exquisite pleasure as his length hits the right spot.

Finally, I have to let the strength of our passion take over. I close my eyes and grip Leo's hands and ride his hips like I'm a professional dancer, throwing power and grace into every gyration. When I feel that tickle turn into an overwhelming tidal wave, I cry out his name.

"Oh fuck, Leo, yes." All thoughts and fears, anything from our past, is gone. It's like my body knows Leo is mine. Has always known this is not just right. This is everything. Every emotion from love to happiness to relief fills my limbs. My brain is even free, free of worry and fear. All I am is this union, with this man, in this moment.

I tremble through my climax, my head thrown back and my mouth open. When I finally slow down, Leo grits out, "Don't move."

He uses my hands and the strength of his hips to bounce me hard up and down on his dick. It's a powerful move and I know he won't last long, but I savor it. He thrusts into me, and my tits are banging against my chest, bouncing and riding the power that seems to be created by our love. We've made love like this before, many times. The move isn't new, but the feelings, the emotions behind it, make this feel like the first time.

I'm breathless and wordless and boneless as Leo explodes inside me. I can feel spurt after spurt flood into me as he rides out his climax. His hands are firm, gripping my fingers tightly. I can smell the heat of his body rising with that familiar scent from his soap. Every sense is filled with him, with us. With this new union that's about so much more than convenience and ease.

This is us.

When he's done, neither one of us moves. I open my eyes. Our fingers are still laced together. His feet dangle off the end of the bed. I don't think I can speak.

He's smiling.

I'm smiling.

Whoever said that being roommates with benefits was enough was full of shit. Oh yeah. It was me. I was the one who believed what we had was fine, good, enough.

I know better now.

What we have together…

This is everything.

19

LEO

SEVEN MONTHS LATER...

"Your father still hasn't forgiven me for knocking up his baby." I'm carrying two dozen rose-gold balloons in one hand and an enormous cardboard poster in the other.

The only reason I know the balloons are rose-gold is because Lia's spent the last six months redecorating Canine Crashpad, and I know she ordered rose-gold balloons one month ago when we finalized the grand opening celebration.

To be honest, I wouldn't know rose-gold from metallic pink if my life depended on it, but since I think this grand opening is a trial run for the baby shower, I'm putting in the effort.

That's how I know Tiny's never forgiven me for knocking up Lia.

He's insisting on hosting the baby shower.

At the compound...

I know there won't be any kids there, but something about hosting a baby shower there takes a little of the badass edge off being fully patched in. I kind of want to enjoy my status in the club for a while. But I suppose if I have to share some of that part of my life with my kids' grandfather, I might as well let him have his way once in a while. He is the president of the MC, after all.

"He's fine with it." Lia points to where she wants me to set out the balloons. "I hope you're prepared to name our son Tiny if it's a boy."

"You can't be fucking serious."

"Uncle Leo!" Zoey claps her hands over Mikey the pit bull's ears. "Language."

I nod my apologies.

"It's like he knows," I say. "He thinks he's king of the goddamn castle."

"He's got to be," Lia says. "Outnumbered by the girl crew the way he is."

She tries to bend down to scratch Mikey's scruff, but she can't quite make it to her knees.

"Zoey," she calls out. "I need a scratching assistant."

Zoey takes her hands off Mikey's ears and starts rubbing his head and cooing. The big beast flops onto his side and sticks a leg in the air, loving every single second of the attention. Pixie, Agnes, and Violet scamper over to nudge their way into the affection.

Bowls of treats have been set up on the counters, and the cardboard sign I brought in announces the grand reopening of Canine Crashpad: Dog Boarding, Day Care, Grooming, & Training. It's a long name, but Lia worked hard to make it happen, and she wanted it all in.

"Hey, man. I gotta dash." Tim claps me on the back. "We got that paint estimate on the Land Rover coming in about twenty minutes."

I nod at him. "You and Juliette coming by for dinner tonight?" I ask. "It's Wednesday."

Tim nods. "Wouldn't miss it. We'll be by after our meeting."

Ever since Tim got out, he and Juliette have been going to NA meetings every day. We have them over for dinner twice a week, Wednesday and Friday, after their meetings. He knew he got lucky when his case was thrown out of court due to some misstep by the police and mishandling of evidence. Supposedly, he's going to keep his nose clean because he knows he got lucky twice, but shit like that doesn't happen often.

Lia insisted on forging some sort of relationship. She keeps telling me family is everything and I should give him another chance.

She's too good and forgiving.

It'll take years, possibly my entire lifetime, until I trust my brother. He's burned that bridge too many times for their not to be damage that can't be easily brushed away.

"Everything ready in here?" Alice comes up behind Lia and strokes her hair. "I'm so proud of you, sweetie."

Lia flushes and nods. "I couldn't be more ready. Can you imagine this place in a few months when I have twenty dogs and a baby?"

Zoey puts on an exaggerated pout. "And a babysitter."

"And a babysitter," Lia agrees.

"You got a minute, son?" I feel Morris's beefy hand on my shoulder.

"Yeah." I turn to find Tiny right behind me. "Uh, is everything okay?"

Tiny grunts and walks away. That's been his

primary form of communicating with me for the last seven months.

"He's going to be fine," Morris says. "I told him I was going to steal you away for a talk."

I follow Morris out to the parking lot. "What's up? Everything all right?"

Morris nods. "I got a couple things to run past you. First has to do with the building here. We got a rental application for a business to take over that vacant spot."

"Yeah? Who is it?" I ask. "What's the business?"

Morris's face falls a bit. "It's your buddy, Arrow. Before you say no, he's not a bail agent anymore. He's opening up a security agency. Private investigations, personal protection." He looks me over. "We've got a brother who may need some work coming up. He's about to get released. Federal pen. Having a business that we trust, right here, could go a long way toward helping out Crow. Helping the club."

Morris knows how I feel about the businesses opening up here. "You think that's safe?" I ask. "Decent clientele?"

"Ah fuck, I don't even think he needs an office, to be honest. I think he wants to work near us."

CHELLE BLISS

Morris chuckles. "I hear the kid's been taking motorcycle lessons."

I laugh my ass off. "Arrow? What, does he want to prospect the MC?"

"Who the fuck knows." Morris shakes his head. "You going to be all right with him underfoot? Near your woman and kids every day?"

"Aw shit." I wave a hand at Morris. "I don't give a fuck. That's ancient history. What's good for the club and the business is good for me. Thanks for checking in with me, though."

I give Morris a half hug and head back toward the store.

"One more thing," Morris says.

I lift my chin at him and wait.

"I'm thinking about taking a weekend before the baby comes. You think Lia would want to do a girls' weekend at my place with Alice and Zoey while you and I hit, I don't know, maybe Blue Ridge, Cabot Trail? Just me and you and the bikes."

"Are you serious?" I can't hold back my excitement. I'm like a kid on Christmas. "Yeah, man. I'd love that. I'm sure Lia would too."

Morris nods. "We'll figure out when and go."

I turn to head back into Canine Crashpad, but something stops me. "Morris," I call out.

He's halfway across the lot, headed for his truck, but he stops and nods. "Yeah?"

"I'm really glad I didn't ride back. I'd much rather ride now. With you."

Morris smacks a hand against the hood of his truck and gives me a grin that I know means he remembers talking me down from running away, leaving everything and hitting the road.

"Me too, son. Me too."

When I go back inside Canine Crashpad, Zoey grabs my arm and tugs me over to look at something ridiculously funny Mikey is doing with his tongue and a bone, which he can't actually chew.

I look around the room, and I reach my hand inside my pocket and feel the red plastic key chain from the Red Pelican. I've been using it ever since Tim went away. After all those years it was a lifeline to him, he handed it over to me for a while. The key I have on it is the key that locks a file cabinet back in my office at the shop. There's only one thing in that cabinet, and I want it locked up for safekeeping until I can officially ask Lia to be mine. I spent a little bit of money on a ring. It's small. We've got a new house to make the mortgage on and a kid on the way, but someday soon, I'm going to make her my wife.

I look over at Lia. She's carrying our future inside her body, and in her heart, she carries my soul. My love. Everything I ever wanted and everything I could ever hope her to be.

Roommate.

Best friend.

Lover.

Wife.

THANK you for reading Broken Dove. If you'd like to know when another book in the series is released, please sign up for my newsletter at menofinked.com/news

And, if you're looking for a FREE and amazing read, check out Flame and learn where Morris and the guys from the Disciples were born. Visit menofinked.com/flame to grab your copy!

ABOUT THE AUTHOR

I'm a full-time writer, time-waster extraordinaire, social media addict, coffee fiend, and ex-history teacher. *To learn more about my books, please visit menofinked.com.*

Want to stay up-to-date on the newest Men of Inked release and more? Join my newsletter.

Join over 10,000 readers on Facebook in Chelle Bliss Books private reader group and talk books and all things reading. Come be part of the family!

See the Gallo Family Tree

Where to Follow Me:

facebook.com/authorchellebliss1

instagram.com/authorchellebliss

bookbub.com/authors/chelle-bliss

goodreads.com/chellebliss

amazon.com/author/chellebliss

twitter.com/ChelleBliss1

pinterest.com/chellebliss10

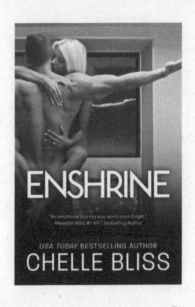

"**Beautiful**. **Poignant**. This book will stay with you long after you've finished." ~ RACHEL VAN DYKEN, #1 NYT BESTSELLING AUTHOR

"An **emotional journey** you won't soon forget." ~ MEREDITH WILD, #1 NYT BESTSELLING AUTHOR

Tap here to learn more about Enshrine or visit menofinked.com/enshrine for more info.